# Elemental

# Elemental

Earth Stories

CALICO

An excerpt from *Ankomst* is published here with permission from Peirene Press.

Two Lines Press
582 Market Street, Suite 700, San Francisco, CA 94104
www.twolinespress.com

ISBN: 978-1-949641-11-0

Cover design by Crisis
Typesetting and interior design by LOKI

Printed in the United States of America

Library of Congress Cataloging-in-Publication Data

NAMES: Kobayashi, Erika, 1978- author. |
Aghaei, Farkhondeh, author. | Gabrielsen, Gøhril, 1961- author.
TITLE: Elemental / Erika Kobayashi, Farkhondeh Aghaei,
Gøhril Gabrielsen [and others].
DESCRIPTION: San Francisco, CA : Two Lines Press, [2021] |
Series: Calico series | Summary: "Collection of international fiction and reportage
that explores how earth, wind, water, and fire shape our narratives and
alter our existence"-- Provided by publisher.
IDENTIFIERS: LCCN 2020037762 | ISBN 9781949641110 (trade paperback)
SUBJECTS: LCSH: Four elements (Philosophy)--Literary collections. |
Literature, Modern--Translations.
CLASSIFICATION: LCC PN6071.F67 E44 2021 | DDC 808.83/936--dc23
LC record available at https://lccn.loc.gov/2020037762

THIS BOOK WAS PUBLISHED WITH SUPPORT
FROM THE NATIONAL ENDOWMENT FOR THE ARTS.

# Precious Stones

**Erika Kobayashi**

Translated from Japanese by Brian Bergstrom

宝石

石は決して死んだりしないし、何もかもを決して忘れたりしない。ずっとずっとその人が生きたことも日々の些細なことも何もかもを憶えたままでいるから。

Stone never dies, and never forgets. It remembers everything that happens to it—every little thing, down to the smallest detail—and preserves it all inside itself.

*From darkness, I shall follow*
*A path into further darkness—*
*Shine on, O distant moon,*
*From the mountains' edge.*

—*Izumi Shikibu*

# 1

CONSTRUCTION ON THE ŌEDO LINE HAD JUST BEGUN. IT WAS a deep hole they had to dig, and there were rumors that a hidden hot spring would be unearthed during the excavation—either that, or, since the site had once been used by the military, the white bones of the war dead.

But in the end, construction proceeded with neither water nor bones bursting forth, and the magenta-hued Ōedo Subway Line—then called Toei Line #12—opened in 1991. Later, a stop at Roppongi was added, which made it the deepest subway station in Tokyo.

The dark entrance during construction—I looked into its depths.

*Way down there beneath the surface, so many distant places end up connected. Isn't that amazing?*

I said this to someone; I was not alone.

Who had it been, standing there beside me?

\*

She looks into the mirror. She's absorbed in the image, entranced, but not by herself—rather, she's staring at the jewel glittering upon her pale breast. Her name is Fumiyo. Her father owns the largest jewelry store in the Mikawa region of Aichi Prefecture. When she married into an X-ray technician's family in a neighboring town, she brought with her a paulownia hope chest filled to the brim with jewels (surely an exaggeration, but that's how she always described it).

Her hair is set into a permanent wave, its undulations setting off her lacquer-black, almond-shaped eyes. She's brushed white powder on the tip of her nose and rubbed a light rouge around her eyes and cheeks, following the "Makeup Techniques for Looking Beautiful beneath Streetlights" published in her beloved *Housewife's Friend*. Beneath the electric light, her stomach swells conspicuously—her pregnancy is nearly to term.

Her mother would say, for as long as she could remember, "Let me teach you the best way to tell a real from a fake."

Her mother is brushing her hair.

"Touch the diamond with a piece of radium. You'll be able

to tell a real one from a fake right away."

Only a real diamond shines brilliantly at the radium's touch.

The year is 1929. The new Emperor's Enthronement after the death of the Taisho Emperor took place just the past autumn.

She turns slowly to look behind her. Her eyes meet mine directly.

And then I wake up.

I've had these dreams ever since the jewel came into my possession. These dreams starring a dead woman.

\*

I opened my eyes and found myself in a minivan. The smell of the car heater filled the air, and soft rain fell beyond the foggy windows. Raindrops hit the glass, drawing lines before disappearing. I followed them with my eyes, thinking, *she was in my dreams again*. From the back seat, I looked into the rearview mirror. The jewel at my breast seemed to give off a faint light. I touched it with my finger and was about to close my eyes again, when my mother turned back toward me from the passenger seat and offered me some convenience store chocolate.

"Looks like I'm going to live a long time yet! I'm looking forward to the hot spring."

My mother was diagnosed with cancer almost immediately after my father died. Her death seemed so immanent that we'd even started discussing what to do with our nearly nonexistent inheritance, but then the radiation therapy worked and her cancer went into remission. To celebrate, we decided to go on a family trip for the first time in many years.

My eldest sister works at a travel agency and procured a stay at a hot spring resort for us. It was located near Ishikawa, in the southern part of Fukushima Prefecture, a place called Nekonaki Onsen—Cat's Cry Spring.

According to my sister, the spring's water is "resurrection water" and can cure any disease; it's a radium spring. The town is supposedly the birthplace of Izumi Shikibu as well, and nearby is the spring—the *izumi*—where she was first bathed after being born, as well as a rock said to be where she set her comb after using the water's surface as a mirror.

"It's perfect for Mom, and besides, it's the cheapest I could find."

It was a nearly all-female family trip with my mother, my three sisters, and me; the only male was my third-eldest sister's son. My sisters' husbands and boyfriends, out of either self-restraint or simple lack of interest, had all decided not to come.

My second-eldest sister ran a hand through her short, bobbed hair as her other hand gripped the steering wheel.

Her job in sales at an apparel company involved a good deal of driving, and so she ended up taking over family chauffeur duties after our father died. As the rain intensified, she raised her voice in irritation as she made the windshield wipers beat faster.

"Aren't there a bunch of places that claim to be Izumi Shikibu's birthplace? I remember when I went to Saga, there was a Zen temple that said she'd been born there. They even had a hanging scroll with some poems on it. And there's a bunch of supposed graves, too! Couldn't we have picked a place a little closer?"

We traveled north up the Tōhoku Expressway past Shirakawa, after which the traffic became steadily sparser as we continued northeast.

My third-eldest sister turned back toward her elementary-school–aged son in the back seat and popped anti-nausea candy into his mouth, and then asked, with a line of worry creasing her brow, "A radium spring—isn't that radioactive? Are you sure it's safe?"

To which my eldest sister replied, touching a gel-manicured finger to her upswept hair, "If you don't like the place I found, you're free to stay somewhere else."

The boy in the back seat remained the only unconcerned party, silently absorbed in organizing his Yo-kai Watch trading cards. Our mother, sitting in the passenger seat with a map spread across her lap, found herself with time on her hands thanks to the GPS and began offering chocolate rather aggressively to everyone in the car.

"Too bad Dad's not still with us, he could have come too."

My second-eldest sister murmured under her breath in response.

"Dad never cared about a hot spring in his life."

Cat's Cry Spring was nestled in the crease between the mountains at the end of a narrow, winding road. Beyond the expanse of asphalt, trees showed the first faint signs of autumn color. Our bungalow, a two-story wooden building with a tile roof, was the most rustic of the various buildings, large and small, scattered around the area. The parking lot seemed vast in proportion to the number of buildings, and only a few cars dotted its surface. The rain still fell, but it had thinned to a near mist.

My third-eldest sister opened her eyes and cried out in relief as she pinned her hair back with a barrette. "Ah, finally—we made it!"

My second-eldest sister murmured under her breath again as she pulled the parking brake. "You can call it 'resurrection water' all you want, it's not like there'll be ghosts walking around or anything…"

My eldest sister grabbed her handbag and was the first to leap from the minivan, exclaiming, "What a nice place!"

A large *noren* cloth emblazoned with the resort's name hung in the entranceway. Beyond it, the interior was dim, but the floor was covered with vivid red wall-to-wall carpeting. We were shown to our bungalow after being handed traditional tea sweets. Several low seats typical of hot spring resorts were clustered in the center of the tatami room. My mother put her luggage down and immediately began boiling water in the electric kettle for tea.

"Wouldn't it be nice if a hot spring like this sprang up near my place?" she mused, addressing no one in particular.

\*

The house where my sisters and I were raised was located in the Nerima district of Tokyo, not far from Hikari-ga-oka—the "Shining Hill."

Hikari-ga-oka used to have a military airstrip on it, and countless planes flew south from there during the Second World War.

After the war's end, the US Army took over the area and built military family residences there, naming it Grant Heights after the Civil War general. My father moved there in 1973, the year Grant Heights was returned to Japan. Enfolded once more into Tokyo city planning, Hikari-ga-oka soon found itself filled with new housing, a waste processing center, and a large public park.

The construction of Hikari-ga-oka Park had begun the year before I was born as the youngest of four sisters, and by the time I started going to elementary school, both the park and the pure-white smokestacks of the waste processing center were fully operational. Soon after, tall, shiny apartment buildings sprang up all around us, and we couldn't stop staring up at them.

We stared because we'd heard that people jumped from them to their deaths. We'd heard that at night we might see ghosts.

My sisters and I were excited at the possibility of seeing a ghost or someone falling from the sky. Outside the Sunshine 60 building in Ikebukuro (built not long before on the former site of the infamous Sugamo Prison), it was hard to think of another building tall enough to kill you if you jumped from it.

So, the four of us kept our eyes on the Hikari-ga-oka sky, waiting for someone to fall. But soon my sisters became preoccupied with shopping and dating, and the time we'd once spent staring up at the sky they spent more and more at IMA, the new shopping mall that had opened nearby.

*IMA*—the word glowed, spelled out in neon light.

I had learned my Roman alphabet, and I sounded the word out to myself again and again as I stared up at it.

I-M-A. IMA. Meaning *now*.

Abandoned by my sisters as they dated and shopped, I kept my vigil tirelessly, searching the skies between the tall buildings around me. Waiting for someone to fall.

\*

The spring gushed forth from deep within the earth.

The mother bathed her child for the first time in its waters. It was the Heian Period, the year 975, the first year of the Tengen era. The spring's water turned a vivid red. The baby raised her voice into a loud cry. She was given the name Princess Tamayo.

Princess Tamayo grew up to be beautiful and clever, her black hair thick and lustrous and long. She always had her beloved cat clutched to her chest, and she could recite poems from the *Manyōshū* from a tender age. She looked into the water from the river's edge and used it as a mirror. Princess Tamayo washed her hair in the river and combed it with care, composing poems all the while. And then she set her comb upon a stone.

Word of her beauty and poetic prowess quickly reached the capital, and before long, Princess Tamayo had to leave home. She was just thirteen.

But her cat could not leave with her.

Overcome with grief, the cat cried for Princess Tamayo from morning till night. It eventually became so weak that it succumbed to illness and was near death.

But then, one day, the cat jumped into the spring, and its illness was miraculously cured.

And so, the spring became known as Cat's Cry Spring, a name that has persisted even now, long after the cat and its mistress had passed into the next world.

Cat's Cry Spring, near the city of Ishikawa in Fukushima Prefecture.

The springs there are radium springs.

In the capital, Princess Tamayo was given a new name as well: Izumi Shikibu.

I read the pamphlet left on the table explaining the origin of the hot spring's name. Exactly one thousand years before, Izumi Shikibu was born in this very location. A laminated map showing sites around the hot spring featured pictures of where she'd been bathed as a newborn, as well as the stone where she'd once set her comb.

I spread out all the pamphlets and maps I'd found in the folder and perused them.

A local historical museum pamphlet explained that the area was known for its veins of rare minerals; it featured photos of the aquamarines and crystals excavated there, as well as, more recently, radioactive ore. The cherry trees lining the banks of the river flowing past Ishikawa were apparently famous too.

Spreading out a tourist map of the greater area, I saw that part of the map was shaded gray—it had been declared off-limits after the Fukushima Daiichi nuclear disaster.

My mother picked up the pamphlet, her mouth stuffed with souvenir "hot spring" sweet-bean cakes, and began to read aloud the origin of the spring's name.

"So, if you take a dip in the spring, you'll live a longer life!"

"Why?" asked my sister's son from the floor, where he was laying his Yo-kai Watch cards out on the tatami.

My mother answered while pouring hot water from the electric kettle into a teapot. "There once was a cat who was very, very sick, and it jumped into the radium spring and got better. It's written right here."

"Cats don't swim—that's dogs!" he retorted, indignant. He fixed my mother with a grave look, and then added, "If a cat jumped in a hot spring, it would drown in it and die."

The "resurrection water" hot spring, where the cat supposedly took its miracle-cure dip, included an outdoor pool.

After eating a lavish dinner of typical hot spring resort cuisine—tempura and sashimi, *nabe* heated over a solid fuel burner, and so on—we began to visit the hot spring in shifts.

I went with my eldest and second-eldest sisters; we soaked together in the crystal-clear, odorless radium spring water. After a while, my sisters climbed out and walked unabashedly bare into the cold air outside, and we all headed toward the outdoor pool. Our chests looked like a diagram of Mendelian inheritance, my eldest sister's ample bosom contrasting with my other sister's and my modest endowments, the only feature in common being our small areolae.

The outdoor pool had a light illuminating it, but everything beyond the rocks and hedges at the pool's edge was engulfed in darkness.

My eldest sister stepped into the pool, wrapping a towel around her long, carefully upswept hair.

"It's been so long since we've all been together like this! I left home as soon as I got engaged, after all."

My second-eldest sister wrung out her towel and folded it neatly into a square, laying it down next to the pool before plunging into the water.

"When I think back to the four of us riding our bikes

around Hikari-ga-oka, it feels like we've become a bunch of withered old maids... On the other hand, though, if this water worked for that cat, maybe it'll work for us too—it'll preserve us like this far into the future!"

I slipped into the water a little way away from my sisters, my towel still wrapped around my body. I followed the white steam with my eyes as it wafted dreamily up from the water to be swallowed by the dark. Tipping my head back to look directly at the sky, I saw a full moon just barely beginning to wane.

My eldest sister seemed to have caught the nostalgic mood.

"Hey, do you remember that urban legend we heard in Hikari-ga-oka? About the man who couldn't die?"

My other sister snorted scornfully from where she sat beside her.

"No—I don't remember that at all!"

My eldest sister was fastidiously tucking stray hairs back into the towel around her head as she went on.

"I forgot what his name was, but people said there was a man who'd hang around IMA—he was immortal, and if you slept with him, it would cure you of any disease!"

"Wha-at?!" My second-eldest sister practically shouted, laughing. "Sleep with? You mean, have sex with?"

"Yeah, that's what I mean."

"You really don't remember?" murmured my eldest sister, absently stirring the surface of the water with her fingernails.

"I can't believe you don't remember. There was that friend of a friend whose grandmother got cancer, she slept with him and then poof—the cancer went away! People talked about it..."

"You go, grandma!" my other sister said jokingly, then added, "We should have had Mom visit him, she could have bounced back faster."

I'd been quiet till then, but even I had to laugh at that.

But my eldest sister didn't crack a smile. "We should have. If it would have cured her cancer, we should have had her do it. I would, if it were me. I'd sleep with anyone."

My other sister laughed again as she began to massage her thighs.

"I'd never. Go to bed with some undead zombie man? Gross. You think he was just a pervert? Or was it some kind of scam?"

"I wonder..."

"I bet it was just a way to talk women into sleeping with him, simple as that." My second-eldest sister was scornful, but my eldest was still lost in her memories.

"I remember all the girls in my class talking about him. In the end, we decided to see what would happen if we all went together to go sleep with him. And we did—all us girls went together to Hikari-ga-oka to find him."

"What? You're joking!"

"But no matter how hard we looked, we could never find him. That's my spooky story."

The reflection of the light illuminating the radium spring undulated on the water's surface.

"The real horror was you girls, it sounds like!"

My second-eldest sister continued massaging her legs underwater.

My eldest sister stared out into the darkness beyond the light and said softly, "Maybe he was never really there at all. Maybe he was just the ghost of someone who'd jumped."

There was a brief silence, and then my sisters looked at each other. After a moment, they both burst out laughing.

I laughed along with them a little before silence fell once more.

I felt like I'd known the man they were talking about.

Who was it?

I couldn't quite remember.

My eldest sister's large breasts and my second-eldest's smaller ones floated in the hot water. I pulled my towel around me tighter and stirred up the water around me. Dark waves broke the light reflected on its surface into pieces.

My second-eldest sister asked, "When was this, anyway?"

My eldest sister thought for a moment, then answered, "I wonder... Someone said—that's right, it was when the Showa Emperor died. The first year of Heisei. I remember on the way to Hikari-ga-oka talking with someone about how weird it was to say 'Heisei' for the year instead of 'Showa.'"

My other sister crossed her legs underwater and sighed.

"The first year of Heisei—that was 1989, wasn't it? Nobody had cellphones then, or even beepers! I don't remember much from that time, really."

My eldest sister sank into the water as if about to slip beneath the surface entirely.

"We were pretty busy dating boys, I remember that."

Soon after, the three of us emerged from the pool, stretching our limbs, and that was the end of the conversation. In the changing room, my eldest sister spent an inordinate amount of time using a special brush under the hair dryer, while my other sister began stretching, still half-naked; I lay out in the tatami area, leaving my hair undried as I drank a Pocari Sweat.

*

The Showa Emperor died on January 7, 1989. I distinctly remember it. As His Majesty's condition worsened, laughter and music disappeared from the airwaves, replaced by grave-faced announcers reporting His blood pressure and the amount of blood discharging from His bowels—I took in more statistics and data about the decline of this person called the Showa Emperor than I ever did about the death of anyone I actually knew. Listening to the litany of numbers, I learned for the first time the real process of death—much more clearly and in greater detail than when my grandfather died, for instance.

The year began but no one wished anyone a Happy New Year. Instead, a siren-like bell rang out one morning, and the television informed us over and over of the Emperor's death. It was a brand-new year, but the sky was dark and heavy with clouds.

By coincidence, an old woman living two doors down from us passed away too, all alone, tucked into her futon. She had lamented her lot to anyone in the neighborhood who'd listen, wishing for an easy death so she could join her mother and father once again. Prayer beads in hand, she'd even started visiting those temples where elderly people pray for a quick and untroublesome death—prayers that, in the end, came true for her. But even when you die quietly in your bed, the police still come; flashing red lights illuminated her front door in the dark and silent night.

Yet no one spared her death a second thought. All the adults around me clutched their black umbrellas and hurried past her door to line up at centers the government had set up for citizens to register their condolences to the Imperial household. The television, too, persisted in broadcasting nothing but news about the Emperor's passing.

Japanese flags adorned with black ribbon began popping up here and there around the neighborhood. Looking at them as I walked past, I chose to imagine they were displayed in commemoration of the quiet passing of the woman from two doors down.

We emerged from the changing area and wandered around the dim hallways lit by the occasional fluorescent bulb, still in our *yukata* and our hands full of wet towels and water bottles.

My second-eldest sister suddenly spoke up, as if she'd just remembered something.

"Hey, where's that stone Izumi Shikibu put her comb on, anyway?"

We picked up a black-and-white photocopied tourist map from the front desk and headed out to search for it. We figured it would be simple enough to find, but it proved elusive, and we searched around the resort in vain for a placard or anything to help us, the steam that clung to our bodies turning cold on our skin. Finally, we came across a small sign for it sitting between two larger ones pointing the way to his-and-her springs named for the god-and-goddess pair Izanagi and Izanami. The path indicated by the sign's arrow went up some stairs and then disappeared down some others, prompting my second-eldest sister to joke as we descended, "Welcome to the Land of the Dead!"

Eventually, we found ourselves in a small garden. There was indeed a large stone there, illuminated by a small light and fastidiously surrounded by a low fence.

My second-eldest sister snorted. "That's it?"

A small wooden sign nearby read The Famous Stone on Which Was Placed the Comb of Izumi Shikibu, followed by a brief recounting of the legend. But that was over a thousand years ago, and now, instead of a river running by to use as a mirror, there was a hot spring resort's foyer and banquet hall.

My eldest sister pulled out her phone.

"This is the Izumi Shikibu stone."

She took a picture. The phone's camera flashed.

*

"Mom, what are you doing? You shouldn't go in the hot spring with your rings on—the water will tarnish the metal and discolor the stones!"

My third-eldest sister was admonishing my mother as she got ready to go to the hot spring without showing any indication that she planned to take off her jewelry. My mother, for her part, seemed not to even hear her and blew a white cloud of cigarette smoke out the open window by her side. And indeed, the fingers on the hand clutching the cigarette glittered with rings.

"It's so cold—can't you smoke outside? Or at least close the window? You really shouldn't be smoking in your condition anyway...." My sister continued to complain, and my mother remained indifferent. The smoke she blew out the window disappeared into the dark as if inhaled by it.

"I'm sorry, but I have no intention of trying to work every one of these rings off just to go in the water. It would take forever."

She very deliberately took the portable ashtray from her pocket and stubbed her cigarette into it, then slid the window shut with a snap. She muttered under her breath, seemingly to herself, "Next, you'll be asking me to take my gold fillings out before I eat."

She likely couldn't slide her rings off even if she tried. She'd gained quite a bit of weight after our father died, and her rings bit deep into her flesh, seemingly on the verge of melding with it completely.

She jammed her feet into the brown slippers provided by the resort and strode into the hall, towel in hand, forcing my sister and her son to trail after her. The precious stones dripping from each hand shone with almost unnatural brightness in the hallway's dimly lit gloom.

Before he passed away, the only gifts my father gave my mother were jewels.

Our household was by no means wealthy, my father having given up his medical career to pursue one as a writer—indeed, you could say we were closer to poor. We knew no sushi beyond the kind that came on a conveyor belt; my sisters and I would fight over the strawberries on the Christmas cake. The expense of raising four daughters ruled out luxury in clothes or food.

Yet my father could never give up his jewelry, even if he had to go into debt to acquire it.

His mother's father had once owned the biggest jewelry store in Mikawa, after all. Making him the son of a jeweler's daughter.

His eyes would light up at the sight of a gem, whether in a department store or a museum, and even when he was dressed in threadbare, yellowed clothes, the fingers of both his hands would be covered in rings. Each set with its own precious stone.

Five years ago, in autumn, he passed away, and his body was placed in a cheap coffin, which in truth was not much of a shock—but his bare, ringless fingers were. Seeing them, I cried for the first time. Though his fingers had swelled so much no ring would have fit on them anyway.

After the funeral, the jewels from his mother—that is, our grandmother—were the only valuables left to divide between the four of us.

The one I received glowed, seeming to give off its own faint light.

And from the first evening I put it around my neck to lie against my breast, I've had dreams showing me her story. The story of my grandmother, Fumiyo. The story of a dead woman.

# 2

The brightness of the sunlight reflected in the mirror from the window behind her makes her squint.

"It's annoying not to have the weather forecast. But no matter."

The trees in the garden outside the window are covered in deep green leaves. *Is the sunlight so bright now because it's going to rain this afternoon?* she wonders to herself.

The radio and newspapers stopped running weather forecasts after the attack on Pearl Harbor. The score from *La dame blanche* plays on the radio, followed by the Japan Youth Symphony Orchestra playing "Silver and Gold," a waltz.

She fans her chest slowly with a small fan. A drop of sweat slides down into the crease between her breasts.

No jewel lies against them.

She's given up her jewels for the sake of her country. Silver and gold, diamonds and amber and agates, rubies and sapphires—they call it "household mining." Sumptuary laws forbidding extravagance have already forced her father's jewelry store to close its doors, despite it having once been the largest in Mikawa.

What will become of these precious stones? Will they be made into bombs? She has no idea. But she does not feel it as a hardship.

Though she can't help thinking back to Manchuria, where she'd gone shopping at the department stores in Harbin, the cobblestones glittering beneath her feet like jewels, streetlights and neon signs illuminating them as she passed by the art-nouveau façade of Harbin Station; she recalls the heavy overcoat she'd wrapped around herself to stave off the winter

wind, cold and sharp enough to cut her ears, and she recalls
the jewel that had glittered at her breast beneath that coat—
and she can't deny the pang of nostalgia the memory brings.

Her husband had been assigned to work at the Japanese
Imperial Army Hospital in Harbin, and they had gone to live
there as a family—husband, wife, and young son.

"I wonder if it still feels like spring in Harbin?" she says
softly, blinking, her eyes dazzled by the still-unfamiliar
Kanazawa summer sun.

The household moved back from Harbin when her husband
got a new job at the Imperial Army Hospital in Kanazawa. This
was but a brief stint for him, though, and soon he was back
en route to Manchuria, part of the medical unit of the 13th
Division of the Imperial Army as it crossed Shanghai's Garden
Bridge into the Foreign Concessions.

She stares at me in the mirror. Her lips, gently touched
with lipstick, slowly part.

"If otherwise the war would be lost and my husband and
son killed, a few jewels are a small price to pay. I'll give them
any they ask for."

I look at her chest; it looks even paler than before. As I do,
my gaze meets hers.

And then I wake up.

*

I opened my eyes and found myself in a subway car. Eventually, I realized I was on the Ōedo Line—sitting at the terminus, in fact. Hikari-ga-oka Station.

Had I really drunk so much? When and where had I gotten on this train? And why? My memory was hazy. Wasn't I supposed to have changed, like usual, at East Shinjuku Station to the Fukutoshin Line heading for Narimasu on my way home from work?

I'd reached the middle of the platform when I put my hand to my mouth and ran to the restroom to throw up. After I'd exhausted myself vomiting, I stood before the dimly lit line of sinks and stared into the mirror.

I looked terrible. My eyes were puffy, with mascara clumped into dark shadows beneath them. I tried to use my hands to wash it off, but the sinks were broken—no water came from them. I had to make do with smoothing out my tangled hair with a comb.

As I did, the jewel at my breast gave off a faint glow.

I passed through the turnstile into the dense crowds passing to and fro as I headed for the exit closest to IMA. The voices of drunks belting out songs on their way home from end-of-year parties echoed throughout the underground passages, passersby swerving to avoid the pools of vomit lurking beneath the splash-marks on the tunnel walls.

I climbed the stairs on my way to the earth's surface and reached a landing. As soon as my feet touched it, I stopped, rooted to the spot.

*I know this.*

I tasted cold winter air.

*I know this place.*

I looked up to the surface from the landing.

There, from far beyond the lights in the windows of the apartment buildings of Hikari-ga-oka, the full moon shone back at me.

*That's when I met him. I saw that man with my own eyes right here.*

I look into the depths of a deep, dark hole.

The Ōedo Line is still under construction. I am young, alone, making my way step-by-step down the stairs into the ground. I take a deep breath—it tastes of cold winter air and fine sand. The faint scritch-scratch of my sneakers' Velcro echoes off the tunnel walls.

I shouldn't go in. Of course I know I shouldn't. Nonetheless, I place first one foot onto a step, and then the other onto another, descending into the earth. My heart thuds in my chest. For what awaits me there, in the cavernous depths at the foot of the stairs, is surely the Land of the Dead.

After a while, even I grew tired of searching the Hikari-ga-oka sky for falling bodies, and my sisters and I turned our attention downward, absorbed by the depths of the hole being opened in the ground beneath us.

Construction had begun on the Ōedo Subway Line. We'd heard rumors that a spring or the bones of the dead might burst forth, feeding our excitement as we imagined the place deep beneath the earth where the Land of the Dead would be. We'd egg each other on, slipping past the tape cordoning off the construction site to see who'd climb the farthest down into the darkness.

"It's the Land of the Dead, so that means all the people who've ever died are down there, and all the animals too!"

"If you eat something while you're down there, worms get into your body!"

"If you look behind you as you climb out, you'll turn to stone!"

The four of us peered deep into the dark hole that had so suddenly appeared. But soon enough, my sisters tired of this too, shifting their attention back to shopping and dating, spending all their time in IMA instead of in contemplation of the earth's depths.

So I was left alone again to peer tirelessly into the darkness at the bottom of the hole. And, from time to time, I'd slip past the tape and see how many steps I could make myself take down into the depths.

The faintly shadowed stairs seemed to extend infinitely into the darkness beneath the earth.

On this particular day, I think I ended up descending farther than I ever had before, having glimpsed a faintly shining light in the darkness. The faint light drew me down toward it, and I felt exalted. I descended farther and farther down the stairs, guided by the light. My lungs chilled from within as the air around me grew colder. My breath would shine briefly white when I exhaled, drifting through the light before the dark swallowed it.

And so, there beneath the ground, in the dark depths of the Land of the Dead, I encountered not the people and animals who'd died before me, but rather the figure of a woman, naked from the waist down, clinging to a man.

The woman on the shadowy landing had her skirt hiked up and was moaning and screaming, tossing her hair wildly as she moved up and down. Thinking back now, she must have been in her late twenties or early thirties. But to me as a teenager, she seemed fully middle-aged. Her fleshy thighs hung in folds and the meat around her waist undulated like waves.

By contrast, the man she clung to struck me as oddly young, almost a boy. He wore a pure-white baseball cap, and his torso, wrapped in a too-big coat, was thin and delicate. The skin of his face and hands and the exposed lower half of his body seemed to shine, faintly illuminating the darkness around him.

One of the man's dainty, glowing fingers was being swallowed up into the woman's ass as he moved his hips back and forth.

The woman sucked his lips noisily. As she opened her mouth onto his, her breath became ragged as their tongues entwined.

The woman moved her hips, first slowly, then faster and faster. Liquid ran down her legs and dripped audibly onto the floor, and then, as if in concert, she began to cry out more and more intensely, as if the man were killing her.

Finally, she closed her eyes and took in a huge breath. Her entire body shuddered.

*Aaaah!*

The man closed his eyes as well and took a deep breath.

And then he slowly opened them.

The man's eyes met mine. They had no eyelashes around them. Their irises shone clear. I stood frozen, rooted to the spot.

Still staring straight at me, the man began to move his hips more vigorously. He worked his fingers between the woman's legs, deliberately spreading her open to show me her vagina.

*Aaaah!*

Stimulated by his fingers, the woman seemed to reach a point of no return, her body convulsing involuntarily.

My heart beat wildly—was she going to die here, right before my eyes? And was I going to be next? The man, his eyes still locked on mine, cried out in a sharp, loud voice.

*Aaaah!*

Trembling, the woman dug her fingernails into the man's flesh. White liquid began to trickle from her crotch.

But the woman hadn't died. She was breathing hard, her cheeks flushed red. Perhaps noticing the man's sight line, she slowly turned her head in my direction.

Our eyes met. I felt as if I were about to pee. The woman looked into my eyes.

"You should do this too, you know. Once you're older."

She drew her lips back, exposing her front teeth, and barked out a laugh.

"Every woman wants to stay young and beautiful, no

matter how old she is. You're too young to know now, but you'll find out."

*

I walked past Hikari-ga-oka Park and headed toward Narimasu Station, turning my back to the moon. A red light blinked in the sky above the smoking area for the nighttime cleaning staff. When had I learned that the purpose of that light was to prevent airplanes from hitting the structure and falling to the earth? White breath swirled up from my mouth and disappeared into the dark.

I stopped at a convenience store on the way but ended up leaving without buying anything. The automatic doors opened and shut; cheery music played. After passing through the dark, residential streets where streetlamps were few, I finally reached my apartment. Flipping the switch at the entrance, light shone through the glass window in the front door.

I dropped my down coat on the floor and collapsed onto the sofa. Empty beer cans and plastic convenience store bags littered the area around me. My cellphone began to ring. I picked it up and heard my third-eldest sister's voice.

I could hear her son reciting the names of the creatures from his Yo-kai Watch game in the background.

"The jewels!"

Jewels?

"I can't believe it—they're fake! The jewels are fake!"

Fake?

My third-eldest sister had apparently found out our grand-mother's jewels, which we'd split between us after our father's death, were fakes. She'd brought them to an expert at the department store for an appraisal and the truth had come out.

"I don't know if only mine are fake, or all of them are—I just know we can't trust anything we got that isn't cold, hard cash!"

I peeled the stockings from my feet as I listened to my sister go on.

"I mean, it's not like I'd been planning on selling them right away or anything, it's just..."

I began to unbutton my blouse. I hadn't turned the heater on, and the cold air pressed in on my body as if to freeze it.

"It's just, I can't help thinking about money. Our son can go to a public primary school, but if he wants to go to private high school later, we'll have to pony up! And I felt Grandma would understand, since it was for her great-grandson, you know?"

I stood in the entrance of my bedroom in the dark, strip-ping off all my clothes without turning on the light. My skirt and blouse joined the tissues and magazines already littering the floor; they bloomed there like flowers. A woman's face smiled up from a magazine cover, her cheeks and the areas beneath her eyes radiant from skillfully applied makeup. My naked body stood reflected in the mirror leaning against the wall in front of me.

The jewel at my breast shone faintly, illuminating my body with its soft glow. I fell onto my futon and climbed between the frigid, stinking sheets. The cold cloth coiled around my exposed skin.

I heard my sister sigh on the other end of the phone.

"I really thought that stuff was valuable, you know? I'd put them in our safe! I feel like such a fool."

I closed my eyes.

Real? Fake?

*Remember this, my child. How to tell the real from the fake.*

*Touch the diamond with radium and you'll know.*

"In any case, it makes me feel so sorry for Grandma. A jeweler's daughter getting scammed with fakes! Ignorance is bliss, they say...."

My sister grew silent on the other end of the line for a bit, and then, as if unable to stand it anymore, she broke the silence with a laugh. "Well, I guess at this point, she's so blissed, she's the Buddha."

Her joking prompted a chuckle from me as well.

My sister's laughter continued for a bit, then abruptly stopped.

"Those jewels had always creeped me out anyway, you know."

My eyes opened wide.

Creeped you out how, sister?

Did you dream too?

Did you dream of the dead?

I was opening my mouth to ask, when my sister's son started crying and our call had to end.

I closed my eyes and tried to sleep.

*

I was still young as I stood there, looking up at the pale, over-cast Hikari-ga-oka sky. I'd passed the age when I'd searched the sky for falling bodies, and I'd grown tired of peering deep into the ground as well, but I didn't really feel like joining my sisters at IMA either. It was March but the air was still cold, my feet numb in their sneakers save for a tingling sensation at the tips of my toes. Only two months had passed since the Emperor's death, and it still felt strange to think this was all now "Heisei."

"Waiting for someone to jump?"

I heard a man's voice behind me and turned to look at him.

It was him. The man whose cries I'd heard intermingled

with the woman's in that underground stairwell. Now that I was seeing him in a well-lit space, his boyishness seemed all the eerier; while the taut skin peeking out from beneath his oversized coat no longer seemed to glow, it nonetheless stood out distinctly to my eyes.

Startled, I almost cried out.

He opened his mouth to speak, as if to soothe me.

"I've seen someone jump, you know."

I stared silently at him in response, then asked, nearly inaudibly, "Did they die? And you saw the body? Weren't you scared?"

Smiling as if drawing his skin even tauter, the man answered.

"I was jealous."

He paused, then went on.

"I was jealous because I can't die."

And then the man began to tell his tale in earnest.


The man told me he'd been born exactly one hundred years ago. The year he turned seven, a man in Europe named Röntgen caused a sensation by discovering rays he named "X" after the mathematical signifier of the unknown; the same year, a huge tsunami hit the northernmost part of Japan's main island.

The man grew up in a beautiful mansion and wanted for

nothing, and his father treasured him dearly as his only son and heir.

But when he turned thirteen, disease struck and he ended up bedridden. His father poured his entire fortune into trying to save him, riding horseback across the country bearing as many jewels as he could carry, praying to every god and Buddha, and begging for help from every doctor, scientist, and snake-oil salesman who crossed his path. But his son only grew weaker.

Then one day, his father ran across a man selling medicine that glowed blue-white with what he called "fairy light." If you take it, the man said, your body will become like this stone, and it will shine for more than sixteen hundred years without dimming.

At this point, the father had no servants left in his employ and had exhausted his fortune. The house itself had begun to collapse, and they sometimes lacked wood to stoke the fire to keep warm. Yet he didn't hesitate to hand over the last jewel he had left, a grand piece of quartz, to buy this medicine for his son.

A few days after his son began to take it, his hair fell out, first from his head and then from his whole body, and after a month, his skin began to flake and peel off as well, with new, taut skin appearing beneath. This new skin seemed to glow, as if lit from within.

And thus, the son attained his form, finding himself in a body that wouldn't die. He decided then to call himself Quartz.

But I was no longer a silly child willing to believe such a ridiculous story. Or at least that's what I told myself, childishly.

And so my reply was a bit cruel.

"So you can't die, huh? Prove it."

Word of the man who could not die eventually reached the capital. They said that sex with him would cure any sickness—typhus, the plague, even cancer. Hearing this, women from all over came to him, opened their legs, and mounted him. A marketplace with souvenir stands sprang up around his house, and elsewhere other competing counterfeit immortals appeared as well. These pretenders promised not just to cure illness but to preserve youth and beauty, too—*One touch and you'll glow as if bathed in moonlight*, as one slogan put it.

But then the war began, and the man found himself arrested again and again. Each time, though, the women seeking to prolong their lives came to his rescue, bailing him out of prison and continuing to make love to him in secret. Even after the war ended, he remained in hiding, passing his days in shadow. But women never stopped coming to him, begging him to cure their illnesses, to preserve their youth and beauty. He met them in that stairwell deep within the earth and satisfied their desires.

The man called Quartz pointed up at the Hikari-ga-oka sky.

"You want me to fall from up there in front of you to prove I can't die?"

I looked up, following his finger with my eyes. Quartz lowered his hand and stroked my cheek. He brought his face toward mine as if to eclipse it, then kissed me.

"I just added a year to your life," he said as our lips parted slowly, our commingled breath rising white from between us to touch the cold sky.

I looked into Quartz's eyes. He had no eyelashes, just as I remembered, and his irises were clear.

"You're a liar."

Those clear eyes, that taut, glowing skin—he was so beautiful.

"And besides, another year means nothing."

What's another year, anyway? What good does that do me?

I wanted to live a lot longer than that. I wanted never to die, like him.

After all, if I died now, I'd be gone and forgotten in an instant.

When school started again, I went to the library and checked out a reference book on minerals. I hadn't believed Quartz's fairy tale in the slightest, but I nonetheless flipped to the entry on quartz.

The photo showed a piece of quartz against a jet-black background; it was beautiful. I learned that clear stones like these were called crystals. The smooth, translucent sides of the hexagonal crystal in the book reminded me of Quartz's taut skin.

Crystal. Quartz.

When quartz crystals come in contact with alternating current, a resonance occurs. They resonate at precise frequencies, these crystals. Around a hundred years ago, Pierre Curie's discovery of this property led to crystals being placed in clocks; crystals keep time for us even now.

Why was it that in my heart of hearts, I longed to believe in this man, to believe in Quartz? That his existence and everything else he'd told me wasn't a lie, that he would never die, that he'd lived a hundred years and would live a thousand more?

Was it because I wanted him to remember me, even far into the future?

How to tell the real from the fake.

But real or fake, neither of us would be around a thousand years from now, would we? Our lives would be the stuff of rumor at best.

I curl slowly into the sheets on my bed. I close my eyes. Awaiting dreams. Dreams of the dead. Dreams of her.

# 3

Her long, thin fingers touch the light reflected on the surface of the water, breaking it into pieces.

With the worsening of the war, there are fewer and fewer chances to take a proper bath like this, and she knows how lucky she is to afford such luxury. She'd had to wait so long in line, and it's so crowded that the tub's lid has been lifted again and again, the water losing heat and growing tepid, but the fact remains that it simply feels good to shed her clothes and submerge herself in water. Still, she can't help but sigh. It's true that it's all starting to get to her—washing her face with strange-smelling laundry soap instead of the imported kind that comes in a red box, sewing five- and ten-sen coins into an endless stream of *senninbari* good-fortune belts to send to soldiers on the front lines. But that's not the only reason she sighs.

Shortly after moving to Kanazawa, her only son took ill. X-rays were taken and medicine prescribed, but he grew worse by the day. By the time the doctor warned that he was nearing death, her mother, who'd traveled a great distance to help her daughter, told her about a spring whose waters were said to cure any disease. There may have been no more treasures left in the jewelry store in Mikawa, but her mother remained as forceful as always.

"Back when the Taisho Emperor was still alive, there was a special train that took people to the spring—it's a radium spring, you know. Everyone wanted to take a dip in it. They said it would cure anything. Typhus, plague, even cancer. You could buy radium rice crackers as souvenirs. The radium makes your skin young again, makes it shine."

She watched her mother as she spoke, distracted by the glints of gold deep within her mouth. The thing was, if such a spring really existed, no one would ever die. There was no reason to believe such a superstitious tale. But she remembered an article she'd read in the newspaper a while ago, in the special edition for the 2600th Anniversary of the Founding of Japan. It told of an experiment conducted for the public at the Tokyo Military Hall in which a famous scientist created what he called a "radioactive man." The man had been given man-made radium to swallow, if she recalled correctly. And so, thinking of this, she sold her very last jewel, which she'd kept hidden from authorities, on the black market and bought a ticket for herself and her son to go to the radium spring.

And then what happened? She took him to the spring, and within a month, somehow, his illness was cured.

*What value can any jewel have compared to his life? I'd give up any number of them to keep him with me.*

She repeated this to herself again and again. Yet that had been her last—after that, she had no more left to give.

She remembers the indescribable joy with which she'd watched her son rise from his sickbed.

After his miraculous recovery, her son applied himself diligently to his studies, and he ended up passing the entrance exam to the prestigious Fourth School. She swelled with pride imagining him walking through the Kanazawa streets wearing the school's black coat, the four-pointed North Star on his cap dazzling all who saw it.

But before he'd had a chance to don the cap even once, he was called away for Student Mobilization. He was assigned to the Inami airplane factory in Toyama Prefecture. Her son packed his things happily, even writing patriotic slogans on spare newspaper like *Brave Students, Join the Special Kamikaze Forces—To the Front Lines!*

On top of this, her husband, despite finally returning to Kanazawa, was now deployed onboard the Heian Maru, shuttling back and forth to Rabaul on the island of New Britain in Papua New Guinea, a journey perilous enough that he'd left behind his last will and testament just in case.

*If I knew it was going to end up like this, perhaps I wouldn't have exchanged my last jewel for a trip to some pool of magic water.*

After all, no one knew when the next airplane factory would be bombed. She should have grown accustomed to the constant air-raid warnings, yet she still startled every time the siren blared. Wouldn't it have been better to die at home, in bed, than on some factory floor?

When would Japan build its own great bomb, anyway? A bomb small as a matchbox but powerful enough to bathe New York or London in flames. Come to think of it, she'd heard rumors that a famous scientist—a graduate of the Kanazawa Fourth School, in fact!—was hard at work creating such a weapon. She longed for him to return to his hometown, wreathed in glory at its completion.

This dream weapon was meant to drop on Saipan. If Japan could take Saipan back from the Americans, they'd no longer have a place to refuel on their way to bomb the mainland, and the constant air raids would finally stop. She'd live free from the fear of bombing once more. Free from the fear of death.

Her body floats in the water; her ample breasts bob to the surface. She sees their small nipples and her breath catches in her throat. She remembers reading in her *Housewife's Friend* an article that purported to tell readers' fortunes based on the shape and size of their breasts. The children of women with small nipples were in danger of misfortune, it said.

*What a disaster everything has become.*

She slowly emerges from the water. Her heat-flushed body is unadorned, but water drips from her breasts like jewels.

Slowly, she turns her head toward me. Her line of sight meets mine.

And then I wake up.

\*

I opened my eyes and found myself in a room with gray industrial carpeting. The walls were covered in posters advertising free new cellphones if customers act now. I was sitting in front of a computer, a rainbow-colored screensaver bouncing around its monitor. A cellphone was sitting on the table in front of it, vibrating. I stared at it, thinking about how even newfangled phones like these had crystals deep within them. When I picked it up, I heard my eldest sister's voice on the other end.

"What are we going to do if Mom dies?"

I could hear station announcements and train sounds in the background.

"I saw Mom in Ikebukuro the other day, and she seemed off to me, you know? She told me she'd been having crazy dreams. I'm getting worried about her."

I kept my eyes on the rainbow screensaver bouncing in front of me.

My sister's voice droned on, occasionally swallowed by the background din.

"I've been thinking about Grandma lately."

Grandma?

"You know, Dad's mom. Grandma Fumiyo. With the jewelry? You're too young to have met her, but I remember her."

According to my sister, Grandma Fumiyo, just before she died, had suddenly started talking about having strange dreams. Concerned, our father had rushed all the way to Tokyo to visit her, but it was already too late—by the time the cancer was discovered, it had progressed so far that there was nothing to be done about it.

"She talked about seeing her 'fourth grandchild' in her dreams. It creeped me out!"

Her fourth grandchild? In other words, me?

I was about to ask about this, but my sister continued talking without giving me a chance to cut in.

"Well, I mean, dreams or no, the question is: What are we going to do if Mom's cancer comes back? I haven't been able to stop thinking about it all day."

Having finally said it all out loud in one go, my sister finished the call by adding, apologetically, "I mean, just—what if? What if? That's all, you know."

The little song signaling a train departure played in the background.

I was still sitting there, staring blankly at my computer, when two girls clutching makeup cases passed by my desk. One of them wore sparkling lamé mascara, and she stopped short and turned in my direction, whispering to her friend, "Hey, over there—what do you think? Real or fake?"

The rainbow screensaver on my monitor suddenly disappeared, revealing the desktop. I froze where I sat, unable to move. But then I noticed that the girl was looking past me at a man across the room.

The man had quite unnaturally dark hair. The other girl snorted.

"So fake. Fake as your tits."

*

My second-eldest sister was driving the four of us down the streets where we used to ride our bicycles together so long ago. At our eldest sister's urging, we'd decided to go together to check up on Mom in person.

Commentators on the radio were talking about how it was the fifth anniversary of the Great East Japan Earthquake. And indeed, now that they mentioned it, the day before yesterday had also been the anniversary of the carpet-bombing of Tokyo.

The white towers of the Hikari-ga-oka waste processing plant rose into the sky before us. A song started playing on the radio.

"This is 'Welcome to New York' by Taylor Swift, from her album 1989."

1989, the year Taylor Swift was born. The year the Showa Emperor died. The year I met Quartz.

Already twenty-seven years ago.


My third-eldest sister was fiddling with her barrettes as she said, "Still, I was disappointed about Grandma's jewels."

My second-eldest sister, her hands on the wheel, snorted her agreement.

"You don't have to tell me—I'd kept them locked up in a safe until just now."

My eldest sister turned back from the passenger seat.

"I don't think we should have the rest of them assessed. As long as there's a possibility they're real, we can dream they are."

My third-eldest sister cut in, raising her voice a little.

"If that's what you think, why don't you wear them?"

"You know I can't! I'm allergic to metal!"

My second-eldest sister snorted softly.

"I can't wear them due to company policy. We handle accessories of our own, after all."

My third-eldest sister made a face as she chewed on her anti-nausea candy, but said nothing.

The car continued its way down the road. Through the windows, we could see the bare-limbed trees lining the street sliding past, interrupted by the park's wide expanses of still-brown grass. The sign for IMA rose on the park's far side, and my second-eldest sister, catching sight of it, said, "Oh, I meant to say—I remembered something. About what we talked about at the hot spring."

She said she remembered now that there had been a pervert who'd show up from time to time around IMA. The school had even distributed flyers warning students about him. The description of the pervert in the flyers seemed to match the description of the man who couldn't die, she said. Maybe it was the same guy!

"He used the same line, you know. 'Sleep with me and I'll cure you, sleep with me and you'll be young and beautiful.' Really perverted stuff like that."

My eldest sister's eyes lit up as she heard this. "Just like I said! So it's not just me!"

"But I mean, how could people be pulled in by that? It's like a joke! 'You want to feel better? Sleep with me! Want to be young and beautiful again? Sleep with me!' What were people thinking?"

My eldest sister's voice was heavy with irony as she responded.

"I remember you buying all those weird supplements when Mom got sick..."

My second-eldest sister exploded. "That's not the same thing at all! Those supplements work! They might have been what cured her, you don't know!"

My third-eldest sister had kept her silence during this exchange, but now she pulled her seat belt to loosen it and leaned forward.

"I don't remember as much about it, but I can't help but wonder—could you really sleep with a guy and wake up young and beautiful again?"

The car crossed Sasame Boulevard. The black earth of daikon fields started to appear on both sides of the road. But in many places, there were newly constructed housing developments where fields had been. The car came slowly to a stop at a light, right in front of a convenience store that also seemed to have just been built.

My second-eldest sister, her hands still firmly clutching the wheel, looked into the rearview mirror at the seat behind her.

"So what would you do if it *were* true? Would you sleep with him?"

\*

The little house where we spent our youth was still the rather rundown structure we all remembered, seeming, as always, on the verge of tipping over completely. A white cat raced out as soon as we opened the door. The inside of the house smelled faintly of mold and was so drafty it chilled us as we entered. The foyer, though, which had always been so cluttered, was now eerily tidy; we exchanged puzzled glances at the sight.

My second-eldest sister murmured, "This is a bad sign...."

My eldest sister seemed to agree, saying in a low voice, "It looks like Mom started final prep, doesn't it?"

My third-eldest sister slid her feet into a pair of the slippers that had been so neatly lined up in front of the step up into the house proper. "Final prep?" she asked.

My second-eldest sister looked faintly irritated as she answered. "You haven't heard of that? You know how there's a set of things you do as you plan a wedding, right? Well, there's this trend now where people do the same thing planning their own deaths—buy a grave marker, write their will, clean out their place..."

The white cat lingered at the door with us, seeming to listen to our conversation as it wound itself around our legs and wriggled its hips to get our attention.

Just then, Mom opened the door to the kitchen, emerging from its depths. The hot smell of the gas heater wafted through the door with her.

She seemed well, not withered or gaunt at all. If anything, she seemed more full-bodied than usual; in any case, she hardly seemed to be in the late stages of cancer, and was full of good cheer as well.

"I bought cake for us!"

There was a small Buddhist shrine set in the corner of the kitchen, and we took turns clasping our hands before it. Photos of various relatives decorated the shrine; our father's black-and-white portrait sat right in the center in its black plastic frame. Next to him was his mother, Fumiyo. She had died much younger than our father had, and so, at least in their black-and-white portraits, they looked like brother and sister.

Perhaps that's how it'll be for all of us, eventually—all our distinct roles as grandmothers or mothers or fathers or daughters lost to time, everyone just a series of siblings in photos. My older sisters rang the little golden bell and lit the incense.

"That's not a good sign…"

My second-eldest sister said this to me under her breath, indicating the white chrysanthemum placed carefully next to the bell along with fresh offerings of rice and tea. We'd never seen our mother so pious. Thin ribbons of white smoke rose from the glowing red ends of the incense sticks.

The cake Mom had bought was a strawberry shortcake already cut into portions, not a whole cake like the ones she used to bring home at Christmas, so there was no need for us to fight over the strawberries. She made instant coffee and served it to us in one too many mugs, then sat down at the place farthest from the door and dug zestily into her piece.

"There's something I wanted to talk to you kids about…"

Here it comes—we braced ourselves for what she was about to say. But Mom stopped speaking, her fingers still gripping her fork, and silence descended upon the table. White steam wafted up from the mugs in front of us.

Finally, unable to stand it any longer, my eldest sister spoke.

"Mom, you don't need to hide—you can tell us anything!"

My second-eldest sister pressed further.

"It's true, Mom. What would we do if you just disappeared

one day without telling us anything?"

Shocked, Mom jerked her hand. Whipped cream flew from her forkful of cake onto the floor.

"It's not—I'm not—"

The white cat darted over and began licking the spilled cream.

"I'm not *dying*. I met someone!"

A man who had worked as a caregiver for our father had apparently kept dropping by even after his death, helping with shopping or tidying up. It became clear after a while that this man had feelings for Mom, and Mom didn't mind him either, now that she thought about it—this is how she explained it to us.

Mom blushed.

"He's a bit younger than me, though..."

She continued, more abashedly than before.

"He got me started on hula lessons. His younger sister lives—oh, what is it called now? It used to be the Jōban Hawaiian Center, now it's, that's right, it's called Spa Resort Hawaiian. She grew up near there and danced hula since she was young, he said. So of course her dancing's a whole different kettle of fish than mine, having done it all her life..."

Then Mom added, as if it had just occurred to her, "Remember last year when we went to that hot spring? It turns out that his father's from there! From Ishikawa, where we went! Maybe we were called there."

My sisters and I exchanged a glance.

"Called there? By whom?" My second-oldest sister murmured this half to herself, but Mom didn't answer. And besides, however strange, this was much better news than that her cancer had come back.

It turned out this man was a considerate gentleman, bringing fresh flowers for the shrine when he visited, lighting the incense, and replenishing the rice and tea offerings. So there they were, explanations for all the ominous signs we'd observed. By the time everything was cleared up, the instant coffee in the extra mug had cooled completely. My eldest sister brought it up.

"Mom, you set out an extra cup of coffee, you know."

Mom rose from her seat without answering and walked over to stand beneath the air vent, putting a cigarette in her mouth and lighting it with a plastic lighter. As always, her fingers glittered with jeweled rings that seemed so embedded in her flesh that they'd never be slid off again.

White smoke curled languorously up from our mother's mouth.

"Your father was a wonderful man. But I'm still alive, and I plan to continue to be for a long time yet."

The jewel at her breast seemed to glow with faint light.

*

My childhood bedroom was located right at the top of the stairs. It, at least, remained essentially unchanged, the furniture draped in white sheets. My three sisters had all left, but I'd decided to stay the night there. A sofa bed sat in the corner of the room, and I pulled it out to sleep on. I stared up at the knotted wood grain on the ceiling, another thing that had remained unchanged since I'd been young. I traced its curves with my eyes, letting them lead me back into the past.

"It's the Land of the Dead, so that means all the people who've ever died are down there, and all the animals too!"

"If you eat something while you're there, worms get into your body!"

"If you look behind you as you climb out, you'll turn to stone!"

My sisters were always saying things like this to me.

I was young, alone, making my way step-by-step down the stairs into the ground at the construction site, a jewel gripped in my hand.

I'd decided that if the only other option was dying, I'd rather turn to stone.

It was a sincere decision.

No matter what sort of place turned out to be down there—the Land of the Dead or wherever—I'd made up my mind: I was going to look behind me on my way out.

Quartz was on the landing, waiting for me. As always, his taut, pale skin glowed softly in the dimness.

"I'll make it so when you die, you'll turn to stone."

I placed the jewel I was holding onto Quartz's palm just as I'd promised. It was my birthstone, given to me by my father.

Quartz enclosed the jewel in his shining, slender hand.

"Stone never dies, and never forgets. It remembers everything that happens to it—every little thing, down to the smallest detail—and preserves it all inside itself."

I looked deep into Quartz's eyes. His lashless eyes, with their clear irises—they were so beautiful.

"Even after a hundred years? A thousand?"

"Even after a million."

"So that means, let's say, if I were to become a stone myself, then that stone would remember me forever too, right?"

I remembered the grand procession of black cars I'd seen on TV. They'd rolled slowly along in the rain. Politicians and celebrities from around the world had gathered to take part in the ceremony. I counted the cars as they passed and imagined that this grand ceremony was in honor of the old woman who'd lived down the street.

"Even if I never become great?"

"Even if you never become great."

His words soothed me to my core.

He didn't tell me that everyone was great, or that everyone was important—Quartz didn't deal in empty platitudes. I took great solace in that.

*I'm fine just as I am. I don't have to become great, I don't have to become my "true self," or anyone else for that matter, I can just be like this and it won't be all for nothing. Even an existence like mine can be remembered.*

"Swear to me. Pinky swear! Swear that if you break this promise you'll swallow a thousand needles."

I hooked my pinky finger to Quartz's. His finger was slender and a little rough, but glowed faintly—I wanted my finger to be hooked to his forever.

"Pinky swear!"

Our fingers slowly unhooked from each other.

"Even if you swallowed a thousand needles, you wouldn't die, so I guess this is all pretty meaningless for you."

I told this little joke and burst out laughing. Quartz's luminous skin stretched even tauter as he laughed too. And then his lips met mine, again and again. My body became illuminated with his light. I let my lips, my tongue, meld with his, just as I had seen that woman do.

But where had it gone, the jewel my father had given me?

*

My eyes were closed but I couldn't sleep. I finally rose from the sofa bed and walked down the stairs. The jewel at my breast began to vibrate slightly as I did. I turned on the gas heater. The white cat appeared from nowhere at my feet, churring softly. I sat down before the little shrine and pulled a few books from the nearby shelf to look at.

One of the books was a history of Ishikawa and the area around Cat's Cry Spring. Did Mom's considerate new gentleman caller give it to her, or had she bought it herself during our trip? Whatever the case, as I leafed through the pages, I encountered headings like, "Ishikawa's Rare Ore," "The Ni-Go Project," "This Rare Element," and so on.

It seemed that Ishikawa's soil yielded rare minerals, including radioactive ore. I recalled that the springs there were radium springs, and that I'd seen pamphlets from the local historical museum introducing the different kinds of ore.

But what was "The Ni-Go Project"?

It turned out that this was the name for the top-secret program carried out under the auspices of the famous physicist

Yoshio Nishina to develop a "uranium bomb"—that is, a nuclear bomb—during World War II.

In 1941, at the request of the Japanese Imperial Army, a top-secret project was undertaken to build a nuclear bomb for Japan.

Approximately 10 kg of Uranium-235 were needed to make such a bomb.

The search for Uranium-235 thus began. From the Korean peninsula to Malaysia, as soon as a territory was invaded, the earth was turned over and stones extracted to be tested.

But 10 kg of Uranium-235 remained elusive.

An attempt was made to bring the uranium from Europe in a Nazi U-boat that crept along the Atlantic Ocean floor, but in the end this strategy failed too.

Meanwhile, the search for domestic sources of uranium continued. The man heading up the search, from excavation to refining, was a graduate of Kanazawa Fourth School, the physicist Satoyasu Iimori. Dr. Iimori had been gathering and studying the ore from the Ishikawa area for a long time, and now a white-feathered arrow had been placed on the map where radioactive ore slept beneath the earth.

Air raids continued in Tokyo even after the carpet-bombing, and the research center was relocated to Ishikawa. Mobilized students gathered there, clearing runways to make airfields on the one hand and digging deep into the ground with dynamite and earth-moving nets on the other.

Mom woke up while I was still reading. Muttering to herself that I'd left the gas heater going, she looked over and caught sight of the book in my hand.

"Ironic, isn't it? Before we had a chance to finish making our own nuclear bomb, two got dropped on us."

She walked over to stand beneath the air vent and light up a cigarette.

"Or maybe we succeeded by failing to make one, in the end."

*Let me teach you the best way to tell a real from a fake...*

I turned to Mom. "What's the best way to tell a success from a failure?" I asked.

White cigarette smoke floated languorously upward only to disappear, swallowed by the air vent.

The white cat cried out loudly from where it sat at my feet.

Mom took the book from me and leafed quickly through it with her jewel-encrusted fingers. She stopped at a page with an array of photos on it.

"I've been seeing these in my dreams lately."

The photos showed jewels of various colors.

Dreams of who? Of the dead?

Of my father?

I was on the verge of asking her when I drew up short.

The jewels in the photos looked like the ones we'd inherited from Grandma Fumiyo.

Next to them, there was text.

After the end of World War II, the Occupation government naturally forbade not only the development of nuclear weapons technology, but all research related to radioactivity. This of course meant that Dr. Iimori could not continue his work excavating and refining uranium ore under the auspices of the Ni-Go Project.

Due to this, Dr. Iimori, while remaining in Ishikawa, ended up turning his attention to the use of radioactive ore to create gemstones.

After years of research, Dr. Iimori had produced a rainbow of precious man-made stones: Victoria Stone, Gamma Zirconia, Sun Diamond, Synthetic Quartz Eye, and so on.

In short, while his dream of creating nuclear weapons never came true, in their place he created precious stones, radiant with light.

Ash fell from the end of the cigarette in Mom's mouth.

"Can a jewel retain the memory of someone's life, I wonder? So if you wear it, you'll see that life in your dreams?"

# 4

She looks into the mirror. A grand jewel glitters upon her breast, just as before, but instead of being entranced, she's brought up short.

The war had ended. The government had mobilized her son to work at an airplane factory, but he had escaped death—before an air raid could strike the factory, two nuclear bombs had been dropped, one on Hiroshima, the other on Nagasaki, and Japan had surrendered.

But she had no reason to know that that rumored bomb of her dreams, that bomb meant for Saipan that wasn't completed on time—she had no reason to know it was the same kind of bomb as the ones dropped on Japan.

The Emperor's voice was broadcast over the airwaves. She heard that voice, the voice of the Showa Emperor, the voice of a man who was also a god. The broadcast kept cutting out, though, so it was difficult to grasp what that voice was actually trying to say.

Her husband had lost his vocation as a military doctor, and he was forbidden from public service by the Occupation government; her family's jewelry business had been destroyed during the war; MacArthur's GHQ had transformed the Emperor from god into human; but she herself remained as she had always been: a jeweler's daughter. Even as her hands were bare of even a single jewel.

No matter how hungry she got, more than dumpling soup, more than chocolate, what she desired most were jewels.

She wanted it all back—her jewels, her past—she wanted every little thing she'd lost returned to her, back to the way it had been.

Quite a bit of time passed following the war's end before precious stones came into her hands once more. No one knew where she'd found them—what department store or jeweler—or how much she'd had to pay, but what was certain was that one day a grand jewel lay upon her breast again just as it had before. The only difference was that, rather than glittering with reflected light, this new jewel seemed to glow softly from within.

But by the time this new, glowing jewel appeared at her breast, her son had long since left home and gotten married, and in fact had already had three children, and her cancer was in its latter stages. Her husband had regained his medical practice as a village doctor again, but it seemed as though he hadn't been able to see the sickness of his own wife.

She's so thin, standing there before the mirror. Slowly, she turns her head to look behind her. Her eyes meet mine directly.

*

I opened my eyes and found myself in a train station. But not an Ōedo Line subway station. This unknown station was made out of wood and seemed brand-new. There was a sign written in old-fashioned characters: Aichi Electric Railway Company. A train made up of matchbox-style cars lit up with electric bulbs slid into the platform. Men and women dressed in kimonos stepped out of the train, umbrellas in hand. A newspaper tucked beneath one of their arms showed the year to be in the Taisho Period. The train began to move again, sliding back out of the station.

Under my breath, I murmured something to myself.

*Way down here beneath the surface, so many distant places end up connected. Isn't that amazing?*

The next thing I saw in this place was Quartz. He looked boyish as always, and his skin glowed softly in the dimness. But instead of a too-big coat, he wore a too-big *kasuri*-patterned kimono.

Quartz was waiting for someone.

A girl emerged from the darkness, dressed in Western clothes and with a large jewel resting upon her breast. I realized

I knew her. She was Grandma Fumiyo as a young woman. On her feet, she wore black leather Mary Janes.

"I'll make it so when you grow old and die, you'll turn to stone."

Just as she'd promised, she gave Quartz the jewel she held in her hand. It was her birthstone, given to her by her father.

Quartz enclosed the jewel in his shining, slender hand.

"Stone never dies, and never forgets. It remembers everything that happens to it—every little thing, down to the smallest detail—and preserves it all inside itself."

She looked into Quartz's eyes. They were lashless, the irises clear.

"Even after a hundred years? A thousand?"

"Even after a million."

"So that means, let's say, if I were to become a stone myself, then that stone would remember me forever too, right?"

She thought about the commemorative picture-postcard book in her house—the Crown Princess in her one-piece dress and flower-covered hat, the Crown Prince in his Mandarin-collared uniform, his breast covered in medals, soon to become the Showa Emperor. They were photographs taken during their wedding, which had only recently taken place, having been delayed due to the Great Kantō Earthquake. Everywhere was still wrapped in an atmosphere of celebration.

Tokyo, the Imperial Capital, was on the road to reconstruction. But beneath the glorious Capital she imagined, deep down at the bottom of its wells, the corpses of those massacred in the earthquake's aftermath still lay where they'd been thrown, never to be discovered.

"Even if I never become great?"

"Even if you never become great."

Quartz nodded deeply.

"Even if I never become important?"

"Even if you never become important."

As she listened to his reassurances, her face lit up.

"Swear to me. Pinky swear! Swear that if you break this promise you'll swallow a thousand needles."

She hooked her pinky finger to Quartz's.

"Pinky swear!"

Their fingers slowly unhooked from each other.

"Even if you swallowed a thousand needles, you wouldn't die, so I guess this is all pretty meaningless for you, isn't it?"

Slowly, she turns her head to look behind her. Her eyes meet mine directly.

*

She handed her jewels to her son, who had rushed to her side all the way from Tokyo.

"Take these jewels and give them to your daughters when I die."

Her son took them in his large hands.

Her fingers were bare of any rings at all. She had grown too thin, and they had all slipped off.

She looked at her son from where she lay bedridden. His hairline had receded almost to the back of his head. He looked nothing like he once did, and this time she was the one too weak to leave her futon, not him.

His three daughters sat clustered together behind him, their heads bent and their bodies small, silently watching her. But his wife was not there. For she was due to give birth to her fourth child at any moment.

Her lips moved almost imperceptibly.

"Remember this..."

And then she fell silent. And then fell asleep.

Her son had no idea what she might have wanted to tell him not to forget. His hand held the jewels she'd given him; his fingers glittered with rings.

Long after this, I realized.

Perhaps she'd known all along.

Known that sometimes, no matter how much effort you

make, it will all still end in failure and defeat. That what you've lost in the past can never truly return to you. But also, that from deep within these depths, precious stones may still emerge, glowing with their own light.

*I'm the daughter of a jeweler. My eyes are hardly fooled!*

She threw her money down as she spit the words, light-radiating jewels clutched in her other hand.

*You presume to tell me what is and isn't "really real"?*

Dr. Iimori's stones were produced in large quantities and sold in department stores everywhere. But a gemstone's value resides in its naturalness, and the man-made stones were generally shunned. Their production ceased in the 1990s, and today, there isn't even anyone left who properly remembers the process by which they were made.

But it was precisely these artificial stones that she yearned to hold in her hands.

I stand beside her bed, watching as life slips from her.

*Watch as I turn to stone. As I turn into a jewel.*

She dies. She is sixty-seven years old.


I look into her eyes. But they can no longer meet mine.

I understand for the first time that to die is to lose the ability to meet another's gaze.

*

She lay in a wooden coffin dressed in white, the money she'd need to cross the Sanzu River into the Land of the Dead tucked into her breast pocket. The monk arrived and began to intone the sutras, and then both she and the coffin were placed in the incinerator and burned to ash.

New Year's Day had just passed, and the clouds hung low and heavy in the sky, light rain showers mixed with snow breaking out sporadically all day.

I looked up into the sky. The crematorium's smokestack stretched up toward the clouds. People's bodies turned to black smoke and rose up out of the smokestack to touch them.

The funeral director appeared, his white-gloved hands carrying long chopsticks and a box, and he began to put her scorched bones one by one into the box. As I watched him, I suddenly cried out involuntarily.

For glittering there amid the bones was a small diamond.

Since human bones are made of carbon, on rare occasions the intensity of the incineration forms small diamonds from them—the funeral director seemed completely unsurprised as he explained this to us.

Her son and her older sister used the chopsticks together to place this precious stone into the box. Her son's three daughters watched intently as they did.

And then I opened my eyes.

*

I stand in front of IMA. It is spring.

The tenth day of the Fourth Month has passed in Tokyo, the shade beneath the trees as they leaf out growing darker with each passing day, just as Izumi Shikibu observed a thousand years before—the world shining brighter than a dream even as the depth of human sorrow deepens.

I am making my way step-by-step down the stairs into the Ōedo Subway Line. People pass me on their way up the stairs into the light: one, then another, and then a third. I reach the landing and then walk down into a dim, unpopulated passage, eventually passing through the turnstile into the subway proper. I descend ever deeper into the earth.

The station announcements and the little song that plays when a train arrives echo off the tunnel walls. A still-new magenta-painted subway car pulls up to the platform. The car is nearly empty.

I enter the car. A rush of air from deep within the earth ruffles my hair. As it does, I hear a man's voice behind me.

"Are you waiting for someone to jump?"

The subway car gradually begins to move. The scene behind

the glass before me slides away and disappears, replaced by darkness that reveals my reflection. A jewel hangs at my breast, glowing softly.

Slowly, I turn my head to look behind me.

# Dog Rose in the Wind, the Rain, the Earth

**Farkhondeh Aghaei**

Translated from Persian
by Michelle Quay

نسترن در باد، نسترن در باران، نسترن در خاک

I wanted to look at the coursing, muddy water. It excited me. It seemed like it was taking things along with it.

دوست داشتم جریان گل‌آلود آب را نگاه کنم. به هیجانم می‌آورد. انگار چیزهایی را با خود می‌برد.

ON A LANGUID AFTERNOON IN TEHRAN, WE PASSED THROUGH the quiet, leafy backstreets of Shemiran and down lanes of upscale, modern houses. As we neared the Ghodsian estate, Father explained one last time, with a frown, that I could turn around right now if I wanted to, that he didn't care if I got married at all. The image of Hormoz came to mind for a moment, in the Rome airport as he nervously ran around taking care of things, lips trembling as he tried to find the words to say goodbye. From then on, much to my annoyance, he'd been calling me day and night. But what could I say? We entered the Ghodsian house in silence. Reyhaneh, the housekeeper, showed us into a beautiful parlor where Mr. and Mrs. Ghodsian were waiting for us. Mrs. Ghodsian was wearing head-to-toe black, which showed off her pale-white, moonlit skin in a particularly elegant way, and she had carefully arranged her jet-black hair in an updo. She barely looked at me once—very cursorily, like I wasn't there. She shook Father's hand, made small talk, and asked why it had been so many years since he had come to see her.

Mr. Ghodsian was a thin, tall, elderly man with boney cheeks. Dressed in clothes slightly too big for him, he didn't move throughout the entire visit, sunken into the couch. Every once in a while, he repeated mindlessly, "Yes, just so. Just so. Yes." The fact that he was a businessman and, rumor had it, very wealthy didn't seem to fit with his appearance.

Reyhaneh brought some tea in on a silver tray and offered it to us. Mrs. Ghodsian bit into her sugar cube in silence, then idly sipped her tea. I heard the sound of the sugar dissolving in her mouth and the tea slipping down her throat. During the hour I was there, no words of any particular significance were spoken. When Father moved to get going, Mrs. Ghodsian asked him, as if she'd just remembered, whether he had plans for continuing my education. After a brief pause, Father said that if it wasn't possible to enroll me in a university here, he was ready to send me abroad, although he had no specific country in mind just yet. That's all that was said about me, and after saying our goodbyes, we left the house with an air of assumed dignity.

The entire time we were inside, I'd been expecting to burst into tears the moment we got into the car. Instead, I started to laugh and made Father crack up with my impression of Mrs.

Ghodsian drinking tea. Right then and there I decided never to go back to that house again.

Hormoz called from Italy as usual that night. He was dying to hear how my meeting with his mother had gone. He almost yelled his question: "Mother didn't behave too badly, did she?"

"Was she supposed to?" I replied.

"No, no," he said, embarrassed. "But she always acts a certain way, I mean, it seems like she... So what did she think?"

"You're going to have to ask her."

I met Hormoz completely by chance in Italy. We'd gone there for Father's treatment, and Father recognized him by his family name. He was one of those distant relatives that Father said he didn't really want to associate with. Hormoz was a young, well-known businessman who'd benefited from his father's years of hard work. A father who now had trouble breathing and could only say, "Yes, just so."

The last few days of our trip, Hormoz spent almost all of his time with us. He said he was lonely. Father asked him why he didn't get married.

"Italian girls are stylish and good-looking," he responded. "They're really great, all things considered, but when you look into their eyes, you realize they don't love you."

After we got back to Tehran, he started calling, insisting we get married.

The day after we met the Ghodsians, Father told me that Hormoz's mother had called him at work to invite us over on Wednesday afternoon. In the very same call, she gave him the address of a tailor and remarked that she didn't want to see me in an outfit made at the bazaar. When I told Father I didn't want to go, he paused, then said it didn't matter to him, that I had to decide for myself.

That night, as I tried to keep my voice steady and rational, I explained to Hormoz that I would prefer not to meet with his mother again, and that for now the question of marriage was off the table. That made him nervous. He asked me if there'd been some offense, and to at least give him one more chance. He definitely planned to speak with his mother.

When Wednesday came around, we went to the Ghodsian house at four in the afternoon. In response to her request, I wore cheap clothes on purpose. Unlike last time, Mrs. Ghodsian welcomed me kindly and even tried to smile at me. In every kind gesture, I could see the results of Hormoz's pleading and threats. Father stayed by Mr. Ghodsian's side while Mrs. Ghodsian laid a cold hand on my shoulder and took me to see the ornate guest parlor. It wasn't a large room, but it had a certain elegance. I hadn't seen anything like it before—curtains of navy velvet with vibrant flowers; old paintings; delicate crown molding; mirrorwork next to delightfully patterned pieces of matching furniture; sets of latticed china that, according to her, were washed several times a year by foreigners; and most eye-catching of all, a giant tan carpet with large red flowers in the center of the room.

As we walked through the parlor, Mrs. Ghodsian said, "I've always hoped that Hormoz's wife would receive our guests in this house." Then she pointed out the red flowers on the carpet and said, "Remember to walk only on the flowers; this carpet gets dirty very quickly."

A few weeks later, in that same parlor, I received some guests who had come for the one-year anniversary of the death of Akbar Ghodsian, Hormoz's uncle. The entryway and the great hall were full of bouquets Mrs. Ghodsian had ordered. I stood stiffly on the red flowers of the carpet, wearing a dress sewn for me by the tailor, and tried not to go outside the bounds of the area that had been assigned to me. Mrs. Ghodsian was sitting in the first chair inside the parlor door, wearing her beaded black dress and natural makeup that showed off her clear, moonlit face. She kept watch over it all without looking directly at the guests.

Half-rising out of her chair as each guest walked in, she directed me with a nod where they were meant to sit, and I guided them in. The parlor was practically full when the sound of a young woman's voice echoed in the entryway. She cried from the great hall, "Akbar! Akbar dear! You're gone! Oh, my beloved Akbar, where have you gone?" A tall, heavy-set woman, she ran from the hall toward the parlor shouting, "Akbar! Akbar!"

Mrs. Ghodsian got up to wrap her in an embrace, but the woman slipped on the marble stairs and fell. Short of breath, with her arms and legs flailing, she kept gasping, "Dear Akbar, dear Akbar!" A few women rushed to help her, while her husband, a few steps behind, yelled, "Take off her corset! Take off her corset!"

His voice reverberated in the entryway. A few people laughed, as others worked to unzip her tight, clingy dress. Meanwhile, her husband, red with humiliation, tried to drag her into the entryway and, from there, get her to the bedroom.

Her face pale, Mrs. Ghodsian practically screamed at the guests that they should get ready to go to Beheshte Zahra Cemetery, then hurried into the entryway to tell Reyhaneh to put the flowers in the car. Minutes later a caravan of fancy cars set out toward Beheshte Zahra carrying stylish men and women and a mountain of beautiful flower wreaths. I was sitting next to Father. The huge basket of flowers he had ordered took up the entire back seat.

It was drizzling, and the sky was obscured by black clouds that grew blacker, closing in on us with every passing moment.

As we entered the main gate of Beheshte Zahra, the rain started coming down hard, and before long it turned into a downpour, combined with a windstorm that grew stronger by the minute. Members of the Ghodsian family got out of their cars, and everyone followed Mrs. Ghodsian toward the funeral hall. Their umbrellas buckled instantly in the raging wind and rain. It was a violent storm that tore clothes away from the body and swallowed legs up to the knee in mud. As rain soaked my clothes and hail pelted me, I covered my head with my arms and tried to keep up with everyone else. Everyone wanted to get to the funeral hall as quickly as they could, but the storm wouldn't allow it. It drove us back, and as water streamed down our faces, we tried again to penetrate the downpour and move forward. Small rivers of rainwater flowed down our arms. The women grabbed onto each other in groups of two or three and forged on. The men held their coats over their faces and pushed ahead blindly. Some of the younger people, who were trapped behind the rest, took the elders in their arms and helped shuffle them forward. I couldn't pick Father out of the crowd. I thought he'd gone to help Mr. Ghodsian and was pulling him along with the other men. The journey seemed endless, as though the ground were stretching out before us, and I lost track of Father. When I finally reached the funeral hall, exhausted and disoriented, I saw a group of people who must have arrived before the downpour. They were waiting in the hall and staring out the large, plain windows. It was an enormous hall lined with metal chairs and rickety tables.

I threw myself onto one of the chairs and tried to rearrange my hair. The women entered in small groups with their hair in disarray and clothes soaked through. Most of the men took their shoes off as they came in, poured the water out, and put them back on. The speaker was at the mic, telling us about the pious and devout life of the dearly departed and offering his condolences to the grieving family. The women stealthily tried to press the water out of their hair or wring out the fabric of their skirts. Thin rivulets of water flowed under the chairs toward the front door, where they pooled into a small puddle.

A bit later, the men brought in Mr. Ghodsian. Apparently, he had changed his clothes in another room. He was now wearing a boyish brown outfit. His trousers stopped just below the knee, and his long, skinny arms stuck halfway out of the sleeves of his jacket. The last member of the party to arrive was Mrs. Ghodsian. Her done-up hair was a mess and her face had turned yellow, like a bruise, the signs of plastic surgery all too apparent. She tottered on her high heels, which were caked in mud, and tried to remain calm. Hobbling and dripping, she reached the center of the proceedings and looked at the women. When the speaker called for those present to mourn—allowing the spirit of the departed Akbar Ghodsian to find peace—Mrs. Ghodsian locked eyes with me and let out such a wail, the entire hall trembled. She writhed in anguish. She beat her head with her hands, tore out her hair, and threw herself on the muddy floor of the hall. Women flocked to her, trying to calm her down.

The hall door opened and in came Father. Ribbons of water streamed down his face. He'd brought the large flower basket as an offering from the car, carrying it gingerly in his hands and wiping his dripping chin with his arm. All that remained of all those flowers were a few metal stakes and green stems. He set the basket aside, sitting down next to Mr. Ghodsian.

The service was adjourned quickly thereafter, the guests dispersed, and I left with Father. The weather was now pleasant and humid. A listless sun shone down. We strolled toward a flood channel that was nearby. Under our feet were puddles, and alongside us the muddy water had risen so high it was rushing past, level with the canal wall. I wanted to walk on the canal's edge. Father said it was dangerous and I shouldn't, but I wouldn't listen. I thought it must not really be dangerous, since the wind and rain had stopped. Father stood away from the edge and took my arm as I walked along the canal. I wanted to look at the coursing, muddy water. It excited me. It seemed like it was taking things along with it.

"I saw a woman's hair bobbing in the water for a moment," I told Father.

"Could be," he replied. "Wouldn't be surprised."

He seemed preoccupied, lost in thought. Suddenly the current intensified. The ground beneath my feet softened and shifted without warning. I tried to move toward Father, but the water was dragging me with it. He had a strong grip on my arm, but I couldn't keep my balance. The water pulled me in. As I screamed, I heard Father's voice in the distance. The water quickly whisked me away, tossing me around and pushing me onward. I kept tumbling headfirst, and water filled my mouth and throat. Casting my arms in all directions, I made contact with nothing. While hurtling forward, I suddenly felt that it was all over, that I could forget about everything, even Father. Then an unexpected calm washed over me.

When I opened my eyes, I was cold. My hair was caught in some moss along the bank of a river, and I could hear the gentle, monotonous gurgling of the water. With my fingernails I freed my hair, then sat halfway up. I was on a wide, sleepy plain. Ancient willows with imposing trunks cloaked the riverbanks in shadow. I thought I would be exhausted, but when I stood up, I felt as though I'd just woken up from a pleasant sleep and was completely fine. I waded through the water, which was clear and shining, flowing with an even sound. You could see signs the river had flooded a few meters in either direction. Mud, slime, and moss covered the willow tree trunks. All along the river, I saw women covered up to their throats in moss, asleep. At first I thought they were dead, but they weren't. Occasionally they'd open their eyes and look at me. Sometimes their hair was so full of moss, I couldn't tell what was moss and what was hair. I told one of the women lying in moss and weeds that I could help her get out, if she wanted. But she said she was comfortable, pulled the moss over her naked body, and went back to sleep. She didn't want to talk to me. However far I walked down the river, I continued to see more and more women lying in the debris, either on their own or in small groups. Much farther on, I saw a woman who looked like Mrs. Ghodsian.

"Did the canal bring you here too, Mrs. Ghodsian?" I asked her.

She said she'd been living here for ages and didn't know anyone by the name of Ghodsian. I came to the middle of a field. A harsh sun was beating down, but the heat didn't bother me. Hard as I tried, I couldn't remember Father, Hormoz, or the red flowers on the carpet. They were vague memories, fading into obscurity.

# Ankomst

Gøhril Gabrielsen

Translated from Norwegian by Deborah Dawkin

Ankomst

For a second or two I feel utterly
confused. There's nothing to focus on,
everything is just snow and sky and sea.

Et sekund eller to er jeg i villrede.
Det er ingenting å feste seg ved,
alt er bare snø og himmel og hav...

# 1

THIS IS WHERE THE WORLD ENDS. FROM HERE THERE IS nothing. An endless sea, edge to edge with cliffs and mountains, two extremes in a relentless conflict, in calm weather as much as in storm.

A light snowdrift fills the air, erasing the division between earth and sky. To avoid any risk of straying too near the edge, I park my snow scooter and trailer next to a boulder. It sticks up from the white-clad landscape, large and black. Hopefully it will be easy to spot even if the snow gets heavier.

The mountain slopes gently down toward the cliff edge. I strap on my snowshoes, adjust my headlamp, and train its beam on each step I take into the graying twilight. The wind is against me. After a few meters I begin to miss the hum and shake of the scooter, conscious of the unpredictability of nature all around me.

I'm now standing five meters from the edge of the cliff, on an outcrop and next to a crevice that cuts into the mountain. A rock rises sheer and jagged out of the sea. I can make out the characteristic layers of shale, the slanting shelves and ledges that run side by side down into the water. I take a step closer to the edge and lean forward. Far below, the sea is crashing in with gray-black breakers. Ceaseless, ear-splitting breakers. When I put my hands over my sheepskin hat and press them to my ears, the booming sound comes through like a pulse pounding against my eardrums.

The rock seems empty, deserted, but I know that storm petrels overwinter there, hidden in the cracks and fissures. I know too that come May the din will be intense, the air filled with the shrieks of thousands of kittiwakes, cormorants, razorbills, auks, and guillemots, and that I'll be here for months, measuring and recording the temperature, air pressure, and wind speed, while I wait for the seabirds to return to their colony on land.

I look up and assess the cloud cover, the light fall of snow that pricks my nose and cheeks. Partly cloudy—or five-eighths cloud cover. Which means there'll be good visibility in some areas and so a chance of getting a connection. I take the satellite phone from my inside pocket, hold it upright with its antenna turned to the sky, and wait for a signal. After a couple of minutes I move, walk a few meters farther on. I try again, holding the telephone vertically, searching, hunting. I go on like this, walking to and fro with my phone in the air, until two lines come up on the display. I take off my gloves and, standing as still as possible, write a message: *Have arrived. Track to bird colony cleared. Weather station and precipitation gauge will be up and working tomorrow. Everything OK. Big kiss.* I hit send, my thumb stiff in the freezing cold. The message disappears. I imagine the words—fragmented, morphed into indecipherable symbols and digits as they climb up between the snowflakes, slip through a gap in the clouds and on toward satellite heaven, to find their star, which in a flash scatters the message back to Earth. Fully legible and comprehensible for Jo.

# 2

The reflective poles that I put out when I drove up the track shine like burning candles in the scooter's lights as I head down the mountainside. The return trip to the cabin goes without a hitch and only half an hour later I park outside. Down on the shore below, piled up on pallets, are my provisions: crates of food, fuel, gasoline, and various pieces of equipment, brought here late last night by the captain, who lugged everything ashore and then, with a cursory nod, reboarded his boat to continue on his way. He's a man of few words, but our agreement was clear. He will return with fresh supplies every five weeks, his next visit being on February 8.

As I watched the lights from his boat vanish into the darkness behind the headland, my isolation from the outside world became an unarguable reality. The nearest settlement is one hundred kilometers away. In summer, on foot, the trip might take three or four days. In winter, especially during the darkest months, it would be plain irresponsible to venture out into this unmarked, impassable terrain. If, for some reason, I do want to leave, the sea will be my only option. But right now I'm not worried. The excitement of getting down to work, of having finally arrived, seventy degrees, fifty-eight minutes, and thirty-six seconds north, far exceeds any possible misgivings about the distance between this peninsula and the sparsely inhabited fjords around me.

The sky in the south is shimmering with red and gold. The sun is on its return journey, so the evenings will slowly grow longer and the mornings lighter, until night merges with day in late April. An uplifting thought. I too shall expand, literally blossom, together with the surrounding nature. My footsteps glint in the snow from the shore up to the cabin. I follow them back down to the pallets, lift the plastic cover, and run my hand over a couple of the crates. Small, choppy waves slip back and forth over the shallows, tugging at the kelp between the rocks and pebbles. A gentle rattling, that watery sound. I straighten up, feel the air fill my lungs, raw and icy cold. What am I waiting for? I should get going.

I've planned it precisely, the physical work. First, unpack my supplies and fill the trailer, then drive back and forth between the shed and the shore until the pallets are empty. Next stack the supplies and tools on the shelves, before unpacking the boxes of measuring instruments. As soon as everything's in place, I'll turn to my fixed day-to-day tasks: collecting firewood, maintaining the snow scooter, filling the generator with gasoline, clearing the snow, and generally keeping strict order, not least over the hours, the days, and myself. The practical tasks must be portioned out, bit by bit. They act as an anchor in a daily existence with no other obligations than to download meteorological data and carry out inspections of the weather station and precipitation gauge. The seabirds will return to land in three or four months. But before that, in just a couple of weeks, there'll be two of us here.

The cabin and shed are surrounded by deep snowdrifts. I had to dig my way to the front entrance last night, though it wasn't deep enough to hold me back for long. A bluish tint lies over the landscape now, and in the remaining twilight I clear more space at the entrance and cut a path to the shed. The shed is the only thing that remains from the few families who lived here in the eighteenth and nineteenth centuries. In the more recent past it's been regularly rented out to hunters and fishermen—as I heard during my reconnaissance trip here last spring. I take off a glove and run my fingers over the outer wall. The panels have been splintered and worn by the wind and weather. The shed door is fastened with a rusty hook which comes loose easily enough, but I have to put my shoulder to it before the door gives way with a creak. I step in and turn up the power on my headlamp. The cone-shaped light cuts sharply into the darkness, revealing plain timber paneling, bare shelves that reach up to the ceiling along one wall, and a stack of firewood along another. Farther in, the beam of light falls on two stalls, no doubt made for a couple of cows and some sheep. In one corner I can see a grindstone, an ax, and a pitchfork. I let the light flit to and fro over the traces of daily lives long gone—marks on the tools, the wear on the timber stalls— and I confirm that the shed is nearly empty and suitable for my things.

The cabin, shaped like an L with a small outside toilet in the corner by the entrance, is built on the site of an old boathouse, with materials salvaged from houses that once stood here. It is solidly built, but very simple, and is showing signs of its age. The kitchen area consists of an old enamel sluice basin, rough-hewn cupboards under a countertop covered in old, cracked waxcloth, and opposite, beneath a long window, a relatively new portable gas stove, next to a rickety side table with drawers. The seating area is larger but sparsely furnished. There is a long plank table, big enough for mealtimes and work. Two rocking chairs stand by the wood stove and two sets of shelves are fixed to the wall, with a rifle hanging between them. Next to the shelves is a window with a view of the fjord. A tiny alcove, separated from the living area by only a simple curtain, acts as a bedroom. A window with a view of the bay and lowland isthmus compensates for any lack of space. The landlord has followed the terms of our agreement precisely: the rooms are clean and tidy, the beds have new mattresses, and the kitchen has had an upgrade, with two new saucepans, some glasses, and cutlery.

Last night, with just the light of a kerosene lamp and the feeble warmth from the stove, it was hard to imagine a practical working life here. But this morning, with the two electric wall lamps on and the generator humming in the background, I could picture us again as I had for so long: Jo and me, together, here in the cabin. Jo engrossed in writing one of his articles and me intent on my research. I imagine the way we might look up, the glances we might exchange, forgiving ourselves for the choices we've made.

The cloud layer thickens. The blue hour ebbs into an all-enveloping darkness and soon there's not a star to be seen. I put down my shovel and stamp the snow from my boots. It's half past one. My first working day is over. I go back into the cabin, sit in the rocking chair in front of the stove, blow on the embers, and throw in a couple of logs. Out of habit, I take my phone from the shelf beside me and check the display. As expected, no connection. I put it back. Not that I'd have called him anyway. Electricity has to be rationed and communication by satellite is expensive. We made an agreement. After I've confirmed my arrival by text, we'll Skype at six o'clock on the third day, and thereafter we'll call and Skype alternately, at the exact same time on dates with odd numbers—that is, if the cloud cover allows. This is my safety net. If he doesn't get an answer or I fail to contact him, it'll be down to difficult weather conditions or because something unforeseen has happened to me.

I fall asleep and wake up an hour later, confused and surrounded by darkness. Still not quite awake, in a kind of dreamlike state, I fix my gaze on the stove door and the light that flickers in the vent. I see myself from the outside, getting gradually smaller and smaller as I grow conscious of the huge distance between myself and everyone I have left behind.

# 3

January 6. A sharp, cold draft seeps in from the window over my bed. I automatically lift a corner of the curtain and peep out. There is, of course, not much to see. The sun is more than twelve degrees below the horizon. I lie still for an instant and feel the contrast between the cold of my nose and the warmth of my body under the duvet. Then, bracing myself, I throw off my bedclothes, swing my legs over the edge of the bed, and put my feet straight down on the ice-cold floor. I sit there for a minute gazing up at the ceiling, until I have made a guess, said aloud to myself: Temperature minus three or four degrees, precipitation zero, a light wind from the southeast. I catch myself smiling as I dress, convinced that the thermometer and wind gauge will prove me right.

The bay lies wrapped in darkness, but in the light of the waxing moon I can make out the waves with frothy white crests rushing up into the shallows. They glide between the rocks on the shore and retreat with a pale metallic sheen. I attach the trailer to the scooter and load it up with the mast for the automatic weather station, along with my measuring equipment, guy wires, and data logger, the bucket for the precipitation gauge, some antifreeze, my snowshoes, a couple of spades, and a gas can. Before pulling on the protective cover, I check yet again that my equipment is properly secured. I don't want an abrupt turn or any sudden dips or humps to damage anything. I also make sure that the emergency beacon and some food and drink are easily accessible in the box under the scooter seat, and as a final precaution I run my hand over my inner pockets to check that my satellite phone, GPS, and some extra batteries for the headlamp are where they should be. *Preparation and caution* is my mantra. I am now ready for what may be my most important trip to the bird cliff. I glance up at the sky. Cloud cover of six-eighths, but no sign of snow clouds. Visibility good. I can drive and trust what I see.

Large parts of the trail have been erased by the incessant wind. I drive steadily, following the reflective poles, accelerating over snowdrifts. On the steeper slopes I have to stand up and rock the scooter to get a firm grip. When I finally arrive up on the plateau, the light beams from my scooter and my headlamp momentarily cross and then shoot off in different directions, confirming just how infinitely vast and desolate the landscape is out here. I turn my focus back on the reflector poles, and any hint of my tracks from the previous day. Eventually, I see the boulder. I stop and turn off the engine. Sweat is running down my spine. My face is stiff with the cold, but I can't resist. I unzip my scooter suit, take off my gloves, and press my hands against my cheeks, forehead, and nose. For a few seconds I feel the warmth of my palms burning against my skin, as the icy wind blows through my woolen sweater and over my stomach, shoulders, breasts.

The automatic precipitation gauge and anchor points for the weather station were installed during the reconnaissance trip last spring. Now I have to find their location using the GPS. They were set up with certain scientific requirements in mind. Only time will tell if this is indeed the optimal place from which to measure precipitation, temperature, air pressure, humidity, and wind speed. The sea temperature—perhaps the most important variable—is transmitted from a buoy via satellite to my PC.

The landmarks that I memorized on my trip in the spring—a slope and a high ridge—have disappeared in the snowdrifts that now cover the landscape. I enter the coordinates and, as I home in on the point displayed on the GPS, I feel a tingle of joy at the concrete nature of the task I have set myself, the hard facts that will now be my focus. Diagrams, rising and falling columns, units, numbers, measurements in hectopascals, meters per second, percentages, and degrees Celsius. Clear and measurable phenomena are what I want. The language of indisputable realities, rather than dumb, undefinable feelings.

I walk a fair distance past the crevice that cuts into the mountain and continue on beyond a wide ridge that extends out toward the rugged cliffs. Here, at the highest point, the wind takes hold and rushes toward me, making me gasp for breath. I move across the plateau, lifting my snowshoes, step-by-step, over the crusty snow in the direction of a south-facing slope. It's not far, but I have to stop several times and look around before the GPS tells me that I'm in the right place. For a second or two I feel utterly confused. There's nothing to focus on, everything is just snow and sky and sea. But as I bring a hand up to shield my eyes and stare into the whiteness, I spot the windscreen on the precipitation gauge, seemingly hovering over the wind-flattened slopes.

The horizon stretches out in an endless arc to the north. As the sea swells between the bird cliff and far-off continents,

I dig out the weather station's anchor points, secure the mast, and connect the sensors and battery before finally clearing away the snow that has settled on the precipitation gauge and installing the measuring bucket and antifreeze. It's a mammoth task, but eventually the two pieces of equipment stand fully operational and connected to the data logger, on a little patch pinpointed by a satellite but calculated by me. The image is powerful. Here we are. The elements and I. Together.

For years I have been waiting to complete my doctoral thesis. As an independent researcher, unaffiliated with any particular university or institution, I have had sole control over this project from day one. The freedom this gives me is enormous, but so too is the responsibility. I had to raise the necessary funding from various sources myself. But I am convinced of the importance of this work; that my findings, when compared to data series collected twenty or thirty years back, will reveal connections that have never been documented adequately before. Findings that will contribute to our understanding of the impact of climatic changes on seabird populations and the effect of atmospheric conditions on their migration and nesting patterns. Kittiwakes, in particular, are now red-listed and considered an endangered species. The numbers of breeding birds have dropped by 80 to 90 percent over a few decades and, as seabirds are indicators of the biodiversity of the ocean, this decline is extremely worrying. That is why I am here, near the bird cliff, at the northernmost tip of the mainland, in the middle of winter, alone. That is why I have cut loose, abandoned everything else for now, because the mapping of these meteorological parameters over a longer period will make a meaningful difference. I have told myself this so many times that I know it to be the truth.

Back outside the cabin, I sit on the scooter, open my inside pocket with numb fingers, and check my satellite phone for the third time today. At last. An answer from Jo. But also a message from S. I open Jo's: *Glad you arrived OK. See you on Skype tomorrow. Hugs and kisses.* I read the text a few times before putting the phone back in my pocket. I can't face reading the other text yet. First I need to get inside and sort myself out. Make myself impenetrable. Strong.

I sit on the scooter for a while longer, listening to the waves, the rattle of the pebbles, the ceaseless wind, but also to the silence in the tightly packed snow all around me. I recall the sounds here last spring: the whispering of the grass in the breeze as it blew across the bay, the rustling in the brushwood as I followed the sound of a bluethroat near a rock. I managed to get right up close as it chirruped away, wagged its tail, and then warned me with a sharp *tack, tack, tack,* followed by a soft *tweet, tweet, tweet.* When I was so close that I could have taken it, grasped it, the bird flew out of the bushes and flapped above my head, round and round. It hurts when I think about it. The courage of this solitary bird. Its nest and eggs were probably close by.

It's almost one o'clock. I go inside and unzip my scooter suit, letting it hang around my waist as I eat an orange at the kitchen counter. Then I pull my suit back on, go out, fix the headlamp over my sheepskin hat, strap on my snowshoes, and using my poles, clamber over snowdrifts and sharp ridges of snow until I am on top of the mountain, some way behind the cabin. From here, in the purple-blue twilight and the sliver of moonlight, I can see the fjords stretching out along either side of the peninsula. A harsh, naked landscape—not a tree or bush in sight.

But as I stand here, I see hints of definition emerge: dips and depressions in the snow, the merest suggestion of shadows, vague angular outlines that mark the houses that once stood there. This scene gives me a sense of calm, of some kind of security, which is perhaps why I came up here. To prove that this place was once inhabited.

# We Have Lived Here Since We Were Born

Andreas Moster

Translated from German
by Rachel Farmer

# Wir leben hier, seit wir geboren sind

The quarry was a white,
protracted hush. A held breath.

Der Steinbruch war ein weißes,
langgezogenes Schweigen.
Ein angehaltener Atem.

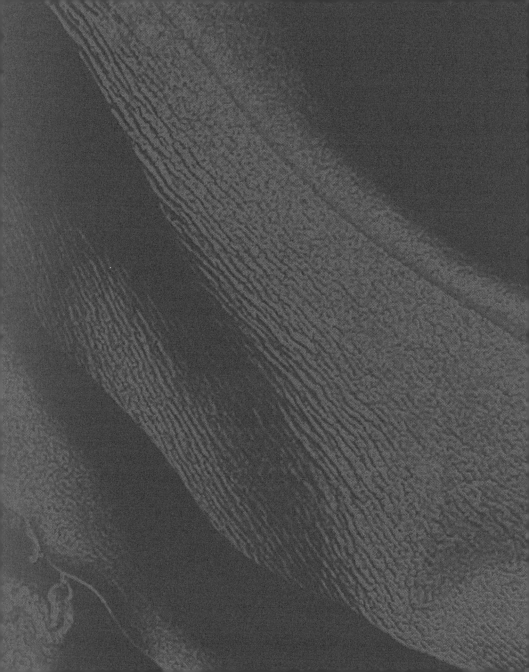

THE GIRLS FOLLOWED HIM AS THEY HAD FOLLOWED HIM
yesterday, and Georg wondered what they wanted from him.
He glanced briefly around at them over his shoulder. They were
taking up the whole width of the path, five abreast, a mirage,
outlaws in the shimmering morning light. The one that had
been with him walked right at the edge, distancing herself a
little from the others by always keeping half a step behind. Her
dress was lighter than the one she had worn in the mountains.
He tried to recall her name, but he could not. Something short,
one syllable, a kind of shout or confirmation. He just could
not remember. After she had left him, he lay awake for a long
time, restless despite his exhaustion, pacing fretfully from
one corner of the room to the other, the flat of his hand on
his stomach, rubbing but, with all the strength that he could
muster, not scratching. His skin had gotten worse despite the
cortisone. He leafed through the documents to calm himself

down, looking at the accounts for the last three years—turnover, yields, outputs, material, and personnel costs. He knew the quarry was just a marginal sidenote in the company's portfolio. Its development was of no great importance; a formality, as he had told the girl. This was his first time making a trip for such a purpose on behalf of the company. Director General P. had entrusted it to him personally. It was probably some kind of test to see how he would cope out there, whether he would be fit to confront the world he hardly knew and the people whose destiny his mere presence would steer in a new direction. His first meeting with the director and the deputy of the quarry the previous afternoon had gone as he had expected. He had laid out the company's concerns and given the director the opportunity to explain himself. The director referred him to the deputy, and the deputy had given a long speech riddled with counteraccusations and, at the end of the meeting, presented him with the latest numbers, which Georg had pored over long into the night. The numbers were contradictory, deliberately obscure. Sitting at his table by the window, he had worked until the early hours untangling the system that was intended to deceive him. The task was, as he had expected, one that required patience but was ultimately doable.

The only thing he had not counted on was the girls.

He turned away from them and continued on his way, along the side of a ditch that ran behind the houses and gardens to divert the rain away into the valley. The ditch was made of the limestone from the quarry, like everything here in the village: houses, buildings, walls, gravestones, and archways, the cobbles on the streets, washbasins, toilet bowls, stairs, stelae, wells, slaughtering blocks. A dull, dirty white, a monoculture that leached the soil and would have rendered it unusable on sight if that had not already happened unnoticed years ago. He dug his fingernail into the soft, pliable stone of a house's outer wall. The nail sunk effortlessly into it and a smattering of chalk trickled to the ground. He had been leaving these little marks all over the place since yesterday, faint half-moon indents from his right thumbnail that would be gone again after the next rain, the next storm, fleeting evidence of his stay here in the village. He did not know exactly how long he would be staying. Several more meetings were planned, including one this afternoon down at the quarry itself, but he felt no hurry, no need to be done with his task more quickly than was necessary. The narrow alleys into which he had turned were deserted. On the main street, he had met several women who had greeted him with a curt nod, but now he was alone with the girls, walking through the hush and the shadows between the closely huddled houses. He walked slowly, completely unhurried. The stone around him swallowed the sound of his footsteps, and he imagined everything else that was in the walls: the barking of dogs and the hissing of cats, the singing of birds, the panicked heartbeat of a hounded fox gone astray, the clopping of mule hoofs on the cobblestones; the wails of childbirth, of newborns, of mothers; the heavy tongues of drunken fathers, a long-drawn-out complaint, the long-drawn-out desire of a body pressed against the wall, a cheek rubbing against the stone, a moan whispered into the wall, children laughing and crying, the patter of the rain and the crackle of heat in summer, the howling of wolves, the howling of a storm, the crushing silence of winter. He placed an ear to the stone and listened. The wall must have been two hundred years old, maybe even older. The documents did not give a precise date for when the village was founded. He listened closely; to the stirring of past years, of the living and the dead. The blood rushed in his ears; otherwise, nothing stirred. He moved his ear away from the wall and glanced around briefly at the girls, who were standing under the archway at the entrance to the alleyway and waited for him to continue. They foresaw nothing, knew nothing, understood nothing of the numbers. He felt a faint tinge of regret; after all, he assumed they had lived their whole lives here and were expecting to live here a long time yet. Without the quarry, they would soon be gone from the village along with everyone else. He imagined the buildings crumbling, overgrown with lichen and grass, seedlings breaking through the floors and cobblestones, animals in every nook, rustling and fumbling from every direction, like beetles hatching from their cocoons and swarming over the deadened nerves of the village.

He cast the thought aside and walked to the end of the alley, which, after rounding a gentle bend, led into the village square. On the clock above the train station building, he saw that it was time. From the corner of his eye, he saw the girls walk across the square to the wall as he entered the inn and went up the stairs to the large, well-lit room on the top floor in which they had spent hours conferring yesterday. The director and the deputy were sitting silently side by side with their backs to the window. He did not shake their hands in greeting, and only nodded before sitting at the table opposite them, opening the file for the current fiscal year and starting to leaf through it. The sun blazed through the window, and dust particles hung apparently weightless in the dense air. He gave the numbers that had struck him the most: a sudden drop in output in the first and second quarter; then, in the third quarter, an equally sudden increase that was not reflected in the revenue. On the contrary, the latter figure had continued to drop.

"Do you have all these quantities in storage, or does the product perhaps not exist at all?"

The deputy's mouth fell open and remained that way for a moment, giving Georg a view of his blunt, blackened molars, his tongue the body of a snail wallowing among the crumbling ruins. In the first few years after the people disappeared, the seasons would begin to break up the village structures. Fall would fill with water the cracks that had opened up in summer; winter would drive in wedges of ice; spring would wash away the loosened fragments. Birds would dash against the windows and shatter them; a storm would sweep the shingles from the roofs; mold would introduce enzymes into the wood of the roof trusses and supporting beams, which would yield and cave in from rot until, after a few decades, the houses lay open and unprotected, overgrown with a tangled carpet of dwarf willow, brambles, and ivy. He turned his gaze from the deputy's mouth and looked through the window at the village square, whose cobblestones would rupture from the fluctuation between hot and cold, seeds wafting over from the forest and the fields and nestling into the cracks. The roots of the young spruces would hoist up its stones. The wall would sag and collapse. The mud oozing down from the hillside would cover the village square and blossoms would spring up, a wild garden that not a soul would enter.

"What is that supposed to mean?" asked the deputy.

"What I mean is you have given me make-believe productivity figures that have nothing to do with reality."

"Is that an accusation?"

"I'm taking that from the numbers you have given me."

He stood up, closed the file with a snap, and placed his hands flat on top of it, as if putting an end to the matter. The deputy fell silent and looked up at him.

"Your books are a lie. Since I have been here, you have been lying to me. You're embarrassing me and you're embarrassing yourselves, and I'm wondering why."

The deputy lunged forward, baring his teeth and growling like a dog. In the deserted village, the dogs would prowl through the crumbling streets, emaciated, frightened, mad, a lost generation, as their offspring would be the first to grow up truly in the wild, free from their masters' punishing, ordering hands. He flinched, taking a step back. The director gripped the deputy's arm and pulled him back down onto his chair before turning back to Georg with marked disdain.

"We will detonate today, then you will see what we have or do not have. Everything has been prepared for you."

He stood up and walked around the table to the door. Georg hesitated. The numbers were unequivocal. Nothing could change them or make them better. As the deputy brushed past him, their shoulders touched for a second. In the doorway, he turned back to him one more time, then he and the director left the room. Georg heard the footsteps of the two men on the stairs, a muffled clatter, growing quieter as they descended, like that of stones being dislodged from a stone wall and plunging straight to the ground.

The girls stood in front of the inn, lined up by height along the wall. One of them was running her fingers again and again through the long brown hair of another. The one that had been with him yesterday took a step away from the wall. Another one brushed the hair away from her face. Georg dropped his gaze and followed the director and the deputy to the station, where another cluster of men was waiting for them in the shade of the awning. The men stood close together, smoking in silence. Thin threads of smoke floated up before their faces. They squinted over at him as he made his way toward them in the wake of the director and the deputy. He did not know who the men were. Quarry employees of some description—engineers, foremen, or simply stone-masons. He stared at them, taking in their rough, chapped hands, their angular faces framed by dark hair. One of the men coughed into his cupped hand. Another turned away, smirking. The gazes of the girls battered against his back, but he resisted the temptation to turn and look at them. The director threw the cigarette he had lit on their short walk into the sand. The men followed suit. One stretched and made a noise, and another, and another. They followed one another in a line toward the platform where the train was already waiting. One of the men climbed into the cab with the train conductor, and the others followed the director into the coach behind. Georg's gaze moved along the long row of tipper wagons that curved around a bend in the tracks leading into the valley. The rusty bellies of the wagons, blanketed in a fine layer of limestone dust, were empty. Numbers and letters were chalked onto the sides—22/136-KY, 7/136-KD—and Georg attempted in vain to decipher a system in them. Deeply engrossed in this code, he was the last man remaining on the platform. Just as the train began to pull away, one of the men reached a hand out of the carriage and pulled him inside. Georg thanked him with a brief nod.

"It wouldn't be half as fun without you."

The man gave him a searching look. He had a thin face, and his unshaven cheeks were sunken, two almost-circular holes, in which you might place two coins as payment for the crossing made by the ferryman in his boat every morning and evening, in order to traverse the stream at its narrowest point. Georg returned his gaze without his usual shyness. The ferryman's eyes were steady, almost looking through him.

"I don't know how much fun it will be for these two gentlemen," said Georg.

He jerked his chin toward the director and deputy who were sitting opposite each other at the back of the carriage, staring out of the window in silence. The ferryman smiled. He leaned toward Georg, forcing him to stand on tiptoe and stretch his neck as far as it would reach, and whispered softly into his ear:

"We had better steer clear of these gentlemen's idea of fun."

Georg smelled the ferryman's breath, hot and stale, with a hint of cinnamon, he thought, or another dark spice. The ferryman ran his hand over his close-cropped hair and turned his gaze to the window, losing himself in the distance. Gingerly, so as not to disturb him, Georg moved away and sat down in a free window seat on the shaded side of the train. He stretched out his legs as far as he could and took a deep breath in and out. The train rattled slowly up the mountain. The last of the village houses lagged behind, isolated, without any clear structure; in the meadows, the summer cattle grazed, surrounded by flies, their spittle-glazed muzzles endlessly chewing, their tails endlessly swatting at the flies that rose and fell in languid clouds. Turning his head, he saw the start of the track that he had taken on his first attempt far below, snaking up into the mountains. The memory sent a wave of heat through his body. He thought about the girl who had been with him, about the beetle that he had almost killed and that had only survived thanks to the girl. He screwed up his eyes, as if from a sudden, stabbing pain. It was silent in the carriage apart from the rattle of the train. The men did not speak to one another. They thought their own thoughts, they noticed nothing. No sound troubled them. They knew the way. The small, dark pine forest beyond the meadows, the trees deformed into scrubby undergrowth, the sudden bend at which the train almost came to a standstill. Only to Georg was any of this new. He looked down into the chasm that opened up below him: steep corridors of scree, and below, an ill-defined, undulating instep. It almost seemed as if the train were suspended, floundering over nothingness. And yet he felt completely safe. Was it because of the men who were leading him? The thin air making his head swim? The fact that he had nothing to lose? His parents were dead, he had no children, and no friends either. His apartment, which he rarely stayed in for long anyway, was down a dark, narrow side street. When he opened the kitchen window and reached an arm out, he could touch the wall of the house opposite. His neighbors did not know him. He could have knocked on their window and passed flour or eggs over to them without leaving his apartment. He lived behind the double-paned windows like a ghost. His mother had died in her sleep. His father had only called him hours later. Georg wondered what he had done in this time. Nothing, probably, just sat there and watched time pass. Outrageous that a person could lie down one evening and be dead in the morning. Never to speak again, never to return. He stared down into the chasm. On the instep grew plants the color of the stone or else coated in stone dust, he could not make it out in the gloom. Slowly, the train gathered speed once again. They left the chasm behind them, the undergrowth dropped back, and the terrain became stonier, a rugged, sun-drenched sea from which only a few lonely blades of grass poked out between the lichen-speckled rocks. Mountain peak after mountain peak lined up in a row across the horizon. The air was so clear that he could make out individual rock formations in their blue-gray flanks: needle-sharp towers; interlocking plates shifted on opposing axes; protruding, proliferating cancers. He thought of his father's words. It is not unfamiliar, it is growing out of me, in me. His father had accepted his fate. A gentle, hunchbacked serenity surrounded him; clenched with the pain at the core of his body, his torso folded forward almost to a right angle, until the only thing he ever saw was the floor on which he shuffled forward, leaning on a cane, mustering all his strength, a laborious, agonizing effort purely for effort's sake. He always walked the same route: from the back entrance of the hospital to the white bench under the chestnut tree, through the grassy dip to the pond, around the pond and back to the bench. Thirty minutes for three hundred meters. If the grass had not been mowed, it took even longer. If it rained heavily, his stick would get stuck in the mud. If it was stormy, he would lean into the wind and fall into the gaps between gusts which would suddenly open up and swallow him. Georg listened to him—not unfamiliar, you can take things as they are. His father's torso drooped to his knee. The vertebrae protruded from his skin. A mountain range, its peaks lined up in a row. The valleys and ridges were all cloaked in a matte green on top of which tiny dots were moving. He tried to keep one in view for any length of time, but he could not. The sudden death of his mother; the slow dying of his father. Between these two ends was a truth he did not understand. He turned to the ferryman, a man who crossed over, who steered back and forth from one bank, from one end to another. Who faced the truth head-on and had to be familiar with it, a fleeting, passing acquaintance. The ferryman sat bolt upright, his back stiff, his hands lying flat on his thighs, his eyes closed. As the train rounded a bend, he moved without looking and leaned his torso to the right, while Georg was pushed to the left and pinned against the window by the centrifugal force. Unresisting, he surrendered his body to the superior force, his arm wedged into the crack of the seat, his face flat against the glass. Forced outward, fleeing, he remembered his grief in the empty house his parents had left behind. He was no longer a son, nor was he a father. No one stood between him and life, between him and death. He was alone. The things he saw belonged to him, the house belonged to him; he walked around it touching everything: the books, the clothes, the pots and pans he had eaten out of, the cellar already piled high with wood for the winter. Forced outward, fleeing, he left the house. It was not easy to sell. It was months until he found a buyer who accepted his conditions and took everything as it was. He only had the most personal things sent to him: letters, photos, diaries. He never saw the house again. He used the money to buy himself the apartment on the narrow, dark side street, opened the window, and touched the wall opposite. A shiver ran down his spine, which was not unpleasant. Alone. No longer a son. The neighbors did not know him. Barely perceptibly, the centrifugal forces eased off. The train rounded the bend onto a straight section of track. The men began to stir. Georg straightened up and looked out of the window where the quarry was opening out aslant in front of him.

The quarry sprawled across the full breadth of the mountain. A wide, rough semicircle, at the edges of which the mountain plunged unsecured into the depths, while the terraced quarry wall rose almost vertically upward, interrupted only by narrow ledges where workmen crawled over scaffolds like ants and knocked blast holes into the wall. The hammer blows rebounded off the wall and rolled back in waves over the surface of the waste piles. Opposite the wall, at the end of the conveyer belt, the crushers ground into four consecutive aggregates, connected in series. The rollers gnashed and crunched against each other, and the stone dust enveloped the crushers like powder blown into the air, covering the face of the machine operator with a thick, white layer. He wiped his hand across his forehead; sweat had mingled with the dust and run into his eyes, which were itching and burning and, later that evening, would be encircled with raw, shining red rings. The machine operator was used to it, and yet it bothered him. He withdrew a rag from his pocket and wiped the dust out of his eyes, while the last grains of grit trickled from the crushers into the screen boxes, which were set violently vibrating by rotating shafts fitted with unbalanced weights. Gradually, the aggregate mix wandered over the grids, danced over the meshes, stood for a moment frozen in midair, before being separated into different grain fractions and falling into the corresponding sacks. The rollers turned off, fell silent. The screech of the drill enveloped the mountain. The workmen cut the blast holes almost vertically into the wall, a hand's width apart from one another. On a long metal table at the foot of the wall, the chief blaster mixed the explosives and filled the funnel-shaped loading devices with the granules. The drills and hammer blows subsided. In the silence over the quarry, the birds took flight, arranged themselves into a broad V-formation, and disappeared behind the mountain peak. The quarry was a white, protracted hush. A held breath. The workmen filled the blast holes with the loading devices and attached the detonators. The ignition wires had been unwound from the red cable drums and entwined together into a thick braid, which the chief blaster attached to the trigger. The workmen fell back, lighting cigarettes. They had internalized the safety clearance, the distance they needed to stand back in order not to be hit, a measurement won with experience. They stood together in small groups.

Silent and waiting.

The chief blaster raised his arm and looked around in all directions. With a deep, swelling howl, the siren penetrated the very marrow of the workmen, the marrow of the mountain. Small animals scurried out of the forest, lizards, salamanders, too late. The siren, the mountain, fell silent. The chief blaster pressed the trigger and sparked the explosion that was meant to slightly elevate the rock so that it would break apart and fall into a pile of coarse rubble at the base of the wall, which the men could then shovel onto the conveyer belt, to the crushers, the sieves, onto the wagons, into the valley.

The mountain held its breath in silence.

A monstrous, seated Buddha, tired and sunken with age into a mass of wrinkles, its small eyes peering down at the men. Pilgrims. Foreign pilgrims stabbing it in the belly. The mountain was awake, startled from another long night of sleep, stretching deep into the day, in which it had walked along the surface of a geometric shape, and though it walked in a straight line, it was always brought back to the same point. In the dream of the shape, it was light, bodiless, and its presence created no resistance in the world. The mountain paused, and the shape along with it. It did not know the shape's name. Sometimes it stood on it, sometimes under it. A faint throbbing came from within it as the pilgrims pushed their fingers into its stone, thrusting in the cold, metal cylinders as sacrificial offerings, piercing into it, carving into its skin, wounding it beyond all measure.

The mountain opened its eyes and looked down at Georg.

Georg looked up at the mountain. Felt its fear, its confusion.

The men next to him shifted nervously from one foot to the other. Even the director and the deputy stopped their whispered conversation, which they had been conducting since leaving the train and which had been growing more and more agitated, and stared at the wall from which hung the wires that stabilized the mountain's bloodstream, filling its heart and lungs. The life of the mountain in these silken threads; this, thought Georg, is what it must be like to wait for a verdict, a final yes or no, guilty or not guilty. The siren howled above them all, warning the world. When it suddenly cut out, it seemed to him as though time itself had cut out too. One last frozen image: the men, small, tiny before the powerful face of the mountain, their heads thrown back, silently awaiting the charge that would course through the red wires into the mountain, each of them the arm's length of a life away from one another, the director, the ferryman, Georg, all the others. The mountain closed its eyes. It was a pain that it knew and forgot again and again. The brief tickling sensation, the sudden expansion, the tearing and rending of the stone. It was old and it knew it was old. Its powers were already disappearing through this knowledge alone. No need for the pilgrims, neither their cravings nor their self-interest, with which they bore down on him and ripped his stone from him to use it for their own gain.

The mountain let out a moan.

Georg perceived it as a separate noise, which pre-loaded the actual detonation with a thought, an idea. He gaped in astonishment. A cloud burst from the mountain, sulfur-yellow and at high speed as if it were growing out of itself, consuming itself, he thought, and that very moment he heard the double blast, the crunch of rock and the trickle of rubble down upon them, and again he thought, this is wrong, this is not how it's supposed to go, before whipping around and running without anywhere to run to. The cloud enveloped him, engulfed him, and he began to cough, stumbled, lime dust everywhere, etching into his eyes, his nose, his mouth, he could no longer see anything, stumbled again, fell down, lay still. All was quiet. Beside him, in the heavy haze of cloud, shadows crept on all fours trailing after one another, dark, sleepwalking animals on their way to the animal graveyard. One of the shadows threw back its head and roared. Another reared up and struck the air with its forelegs before falling to the ground. Georg tried to get to his feet too, to follow the herd. The explosion was still resounding in his head, and he lost his balance, staggering to the left, away from the herd. A hand was laid on his shoulder and he looked up. In a face white with dust shone the blue eyes of the ferryman. His mouth opened into a smile, then he said something Georg could not understand. He took the hand that the ferryman reached out to him and used it to help him straighten up. The ferryman spoke again, louder, practically shouting into his ear.

"...all right?"

Georg stretched out his arms. The world as he knew it strained between his fingers, a random arrangement of things and people. He nodded.

"I'm all right," he said to the ferryman and let his arms fall to his sides.

All around them, the other men were getting to their feet, groaning. The explosion had shrouded them all in white dust so that they could hardly tell each other apart. Coughing, white-haired old men, stooped and disorientated like after a great war. They looked at each other questioningly; no one said a word.

Then came the howling.

The men listened. The howling grew, reverberating off the wall, duplicating and careering back at them from two different directions, the sound of a dog, thought Georg, covering his ears. The howling stopped, and the men straightened up fully. As if the shock of the sound had restored them to themselves again, he could now recognize individual faces again. The ferryman squinted in the direction from which the howling had come. The deputy's jaw was grinding jerkily beneath his thin skin. The director rubbed his cheeks with his hands, again and again.

"What happened?" he asked.

"I told you what might happen," said the deputy.

They stood in a group of eight or nine at the very edge of the expanse of rubble, which radiated out from the wall into the quarry. Everything was coated in a fine layer of dust and aggregate; a quiet trickle could still be heard from the crushers and sieves; on the terraces, the fresh debris was piled up in coarse chunks of varying sizes, which stood at acute angles to each other. Georg tried to make out the lesions in the rock, but the cloud of smoke that hung in the stagnant air in front of the wall blocked his view. He rubbed his eyes. At the base of the wall he recognized the crushed table belonging to the chief blaster, to the right of which, a short distance away, crouched a group of workmen in a circle as if in prayer. The howling sliced the air into uneven fragments. By the wall, the workmen threw their hands in the air. Georg looked at the ferryman, who appeared to wink at him before setting off at a run. The others followed him close behind: the deputy, the director, finally he himself. When he reached the group, he was completely out of breath. The thin, dusty air burned in his lungs, but he forced himself to stand upright and look over the heads of the others toward the man who lay in the middle of them.

The man lay prone with his head turned to the left. His right arm was covered up to the elbow with a huge boulder. Blood spilled out in the shape of a triangle. Everything was white; only the blood was red. In the places where tears and sweat were running over the man's face, his skin was brown. The man howled through his closed mouth. One of the workmen who had drilled the blast holes was holding his left hand. The ferryman tugged his belt free from his pants and tied it around the man's right upper arm.

"We need to turn him over."

"We cannot turn him over."

The man opened his mouth and the howling stopped. He knew it before the others. He threw himself over with a few jerky movements, tearing at the last remaining fibers, coming to lie on his side, then finally on his back. His eyes flickered, seeking out his right arm, which had been left behind under the boulder. One of the workmen took off his shirt and pressed it onto the bloody stump. The man shrieked like a child.

"We need a stretcher."

Two of the workmen ran over to the small hut at the edge of the quarry and returned with a stretcher made from thick cloth. The man stared at his right arm that had been left behind under the boulder. When they lifted him onto the stretcher, he gripped the ferryman's hand and pulled him down to his level.

"Don't forget my arm."

The ferryman squeezed the man's hand and nodded.

"Take him to the train," the director shouted.

Four of the workmen lifted the stretcher and carried the man away. A fifth held his shirt pressed against the stump.

"Take him into the valley," the director shouted. "And send back the second train for us."

Georg did not look at the workmen carrying the stretcher onto the train or the train starting to move off. Nor did he look at the arm that had been left behind under the boulder.

Georg looked up at the mountain.

In the wall, in the belly of the mountain, gaped a great, jagged hole. The cloud of smoke had dispersed. He made out the pattern of the blast holes, a horseshoe open at the bottom, with a thick granite slab arching over the upper curve. The breath of the mountain was shallow as if it had only recently dozed off into a fretful sleep. Georg felt the exhaustion, the need for rest. The sleep of the wounded, from which the mountain would awaken weakened, emaciated by deprivation, much older and continuing to age, practically immortal, its northern flank a victim of wind and erosion.

Georg turned away.

He stood a little apart from the remaining men, among whom a heated discussion had broken out. The deputy's voice in particular burst out again and again in shrill, sharply rising cascades.

"Because of him. All because of him!"

The deputy took a couple of quick steps toward him and punched him full in the face with his fist. Georg fell to the ground. The sky was a cheerful blue once again. Fine wisps of cloud floated across his field of vision and drifted away in the balmy air, warmed by the quarry. The men's legs formed a ring around him, a cage closed in on all sides. Narrow beams of sunlight broke through the close-set bars; the bent upper bodies formed a dome under which the air was blocked in and quickly became stifling. He smelled the men's sweat, no longer able to tell them apart. Their faces swam over him against the light, their faces swaying slightly back and forth. They breathed quietly down upon him. A heaviness overcame him, as if he were lying buried alive under a pile of waste material from the quarry. He listened to the crunching of the boots on the limestone, the rustling of clothes rubbing together. The men closed ranks even further.

Darkness descended upon him.

Beneath him, deep in the rock, the heart of the mountain beat more steadily. The first dream of the new night. On the horizon, the shape, whose name it did not know, rose up, detached itself from the ground, became solid at the edges. With a sigh, the mountain set off. It walked in a straight line without creating any resistance in the world. Just before it reached the shape, it stopped. The pilgrims had gone.

The mountain breathed out.

Smiling, it took a step onto the shape's surface.

# Lalana

**Michèle Rakotoson**

Translated from French by Allison M. Charette

Lalana

The area has been explored, exploited, then ravaged, a strange space, charred space, memory broken by man's will to burn everything behind him.

L'espace a été exploré, exploité, puis ravagé, espace étrange, calciné, mémoire brisée par la volonté de l'homme de tout brûler derrière lui.

HE STANDS THERE, MOTIONLESS, CAUGHT IN THE TANGLE OF
that moment and a vague feeling of fear and trepidation.
If he's not careful, he'll end up being stuck there, too, in
Rivo's in-between space. Spinning between life and death.
Slowly leaning toward the unknown. And it feels like everything around them is affected: the transfixing silence of
this deserted road, the bare gray-blue hills, silhouettes
of the few trees that managed to survive the slash-and-
burning, and the first rice fields marking where the countryside begins.

And yet, that's to be expected from this landscape, there
outside the limits of Antananarivo, with its rice fields, smaller
houses, and kerosene lamps and candleholders in the roadside
stalls, all signs of entering the countryside. Nothing there but
the same mundane things. He must be transmuting his malaise
onto them.

A taxi-brousse flies by, stuffed to bursting: an old, patched-up rust bucket, held together God only knows how, steel hanging by a thread, with its cargo of shabby country folk. The mini-bus hurtles past with clanging metal and a cloud of dust that makes Naivo cough. When the emptiness and silence return, a feeling remains: dozens of eyes still staring at them, unblinking.

"Beware of the wheezing, that's how it starts."

Starts? To say that he jumps when Rivo touches him would be an understatement. His friend has climbed noiselessly out of the car to stand next to him, still trembling. Naivo can hear his breathing, ragged, strangled, strained.

"I need to go pee."

So what? Does he need to be put on the pot, have his fly unzipped?

Rivo is shivering, his hands clutching his waistband. It's slipping, the belt seems enormous, like his wrists, his knuckles, his eyes bulging out of his face.

"Help me." He looks at him, realizes if he doesn't act very quickly, Rivo is going to go in his pants, the illness has reached that point, his sphincter can't hold it anymore… He tosses his just-lit cigarette to the ground. A locust lands on the hood of the car, disoriented, as gray as the sun-scorched bozaka grass and just as ancient, outlasting every disaster. Naivo feels the animal's eyes looking at him before it jumps away. The hood is burning hot.

"Valalan'amboa, na ny tompony aza tsy tia," he thinks, "Damn grasshopper, even the one it's meant for doesn't want it..." With a wry smile, he thinks to himself how, truly, everything is becoming a symbol to him. Only these creatures can survive this devastated landscape, and they must be destroyed, they can't be left to multiply. The insect has disappeared, it left not even a trace of its passing. Naivo stops thinking and opens his friend's belt buckle, unbuttons his pants so he doesn't piss himself, and jumps... Rivo's penis seems so tiny, as if it has shriveled up, blackened like a burnt grasshopper. "Reraka ny sompangan-dry zalahy," he thinks, with what's left of a jeer, "The guy's green grasshopper is shot." There really isn't anything left of the handsome talisman that boys are so proud of, of that member women used to speak so highly of in their veiled terms, sompanga, valala. His fine specimen has become a tiny, crippled thing. AIDS has shot him down midflight, mid-heart, mid-sex.

He takes out another cigarette, instinctively counts how many are left in the box, wonders where he can get some more on the road, and lights it, inhaling slowly, to feel the smoke pervade his throat, then his lungs, burning his mucous membranes, leaving behind an acrid taste, and that scent of leaves. He likes tobacco's headiness, the feeling of his heart, the pulse of his blood quickening, and especially loves the movement, two fingers toward his mouth, against his lips, as he slowly inhales the cigarette like suckling a mother's breast.

"Izay sitrakao ry Raiko..."

And this hymn in his head that will not stop.

"May your will be done, my God..."

Abruptly, Naivo gets the feeling that the landscape is even more arid, the rice fields even more empty, the houses scattered. This landscape, it's protestant, too, austere and harsh like the religion, a religion without pardon or mercy... The world of a severe, omnipresent God. Here, every village, every hamlet has its churches, both Protestant and Catholic, everyone lives in terror of sins committed or in the process of being so, sins to atone for in any case. That's why he and Rivo, they're here, on this road, looking for the Queen's road, in search of the sea and redemption. But what mercy is there for AIDS?

And Naivo, what did he actually say, that day, standing as he was, leaning on the hood of the car, smoking his cigarette, to ward off his fatigue? "Mangala aina kely," his family always told him, "Live a little, rest a little... You have to slow down, face things head on, look at them without panicking..." He straightens and begins to breathe, slowly, to relax. Everything seems calm, actually. He merely has to change the way he looks at things, at the world.

He smokes the last breath of his cigarette. It's as if the horizon has expanded, the countryside is pretty, or all around him, at least...

"Do you remember that village up there?"

Naivo jumps. Rivo's voice is stronger, far from his recent mumbling that had been so hard to make out.

"Weren't you the one who told me the story of that pastor who barricaded himself inside the village when the French came, who starved to death there, he and his whole family?"

Antananarivo is behind them now, a few dozen kilometers away. They're just outside Ambohimangakely, the little blue hill, the very edge of civilization. Houses poke out from the top of the hill.

"We went up there one time with Monsieur Ravoajanahary, remember him?"

Of course he remembers him, he was their mentor, he taught them about every hill, every hamlet, tracing back through the history of kings and, by allusion, the Malagasy people. Naivo is about to say so when Rivo says:

"And you remember the trip to Ambohijoky?"

"You ended up so wasted you threw up."

"Some of my ancestors are from Ambohijoky."

"Oh yeah?"

"They've been described as slaves, but the Merina kingdom

was built because of them, they provided warriors for the king, even the women took part in battles."

There, the word has finally been spoken. Rivo had never talked about that, he'd never mentioned his ancestors. Now he smirks a little, just like he has every other time he's heard about Malagasy history, and kings, and lords. Naivo expects his friend to start in on his hair, as always, an obsession, the forsworn hereditary trait, but Rivo keeps going:

"Ten years from now, there won't be anything left of all this, there'll be houses, and villas, and roads, the rice fields will be filled in, there won't be any more carts, or zebus, and I won't be here."

He sneers as he says it, then adds:

"Here, nothing has grown for a long time. Eucalyptus maybe, possibly mimosa, nothing else. The soil has run off down below, where the rice fields are, but now they're going to be filled in and houses will be built instead, because the water has gone..."

He gets in the car, slowly sits down, and changes the cassette tape, puts on some hira gasy. And the atmosphere changes. The creaky sound of poorly tuned violins fills the car, accompanied by the nasal and slightly out-of-tune country singers, and then the narrator's introduction comes in. Everything follows a pattern in these country operas, even the speeches.

"Ladies and gentlemen," he says, "you who are gathered in this place, here we are, Andohavary people, we have come as friends, as neighbors, not to attack you, nor impose anything upon you, but we have come to talk with you, to propose an ongoing conversation, a time of communal reflection, for life can flow smoothly only when we take this moment for exchange, difficulties can be overcome only when the entire family works together to see every facet of the problem..."

And the patriarch's voice booms out, for the patriarch alone may speak, accompanied by the women's responses at important moments. They speak of life, death, illness, and poverty, expounding upon the need for wisdom and surrender before the will of the presumptive God, anticipating recognition at the end and reward in life beyond, alternating between speeches and resigned songs, the will to resist and to survive, words heard in churches, sermons, restated here. Naivo starts to wish he could turn the tape off and finally have some silence, when Rivo begins murmuring again, his voice becoming clearer and clearer, parodying the rhythm of the hira gasy words:

"Ladies and gentlemen, girls and boys, here we are before you, presenting ourselves before you, heads bowed, we are defeated, the city has defeated us, we have no more rice fields, no more crops, God has forgotten us or wants nothing more to do with us. We of kinky hair, we are defeated and the gates of heaven have closed, but we Blacks, we are as tough as our hair, we will withstand everything, like our hair, and we no longer want to atone for faults that are not our own. Where smooth hair falls, ours will remain, thick, kinky, and persevering. Kinky hair, thick hair, resistant, fierce."

His voice drones on, monotonous, incantatory, then more and more violent, aggressive. The same melodic line, with tonal ruptures now and then, and breaks, and cracks, then cries. It continues for a while, like the voices of the possessed when entering a trance, then Rivo starts tapping his finger on the dashboard in rhythm, in time with his words.

"We have come to see you," Rivo says, speaking loudly to drown out the narrator's voice on the cassette, "to talk of curses, to forswear this curse and talk to you now of laughter and revolution. God is dead and we will sing, he has dragged us down with him and we will dance, may there be condemnation and also life."

He sings louder and louder, practically gasping. His voice cracks, the voice of an old man who is so tired. It's haunting to hear him quivering, sweating, and perhaps even more stunning to see his thin fingers keeping time on the dashboard.

Light a cigarette, he has to light a cigarette. It takes some time for Naivo to find the lighter. Ghosts again, impossible to speak... And then abruptly he realizes the underlying reason for his malaise: he has entered into Rivo's delirium, thinking he hears voices, feeling oppressive presences, breaths, in the car. It's odd, this sense of weight on his chest, this kind of prescience of other things. As a child, he would have been told: "Burn some hair, snap a record, the ancestors are coming back, they have to stay where they are." But adulthood compels logic, and he's not here to become crazy with Rivo or to enter the realm of the dead with him, he's here to go to the sea, to fulfill his friend's final wish. He turns away, drives a little slower to look at the landscape. Laterite bursts up all around, even through tilled soil. It has let itself slide and become hard, dry, as tough as the exposed rock that lends its rough tone to this landscape, barely softened by the dark green of the eucalyptus. It's the color of tomb dust specifically, from the disintegrating bodies. The rice fields in minuscule valleys are going yellow and the ears have turned the pale, flat green color of early paddy rice in need of culling. This landscape is dry, desperately dry, and just looking at it can parch the mucous membranes. And on top of that, it's extremely hot in the car. They'd turned off the air-conditioning because it makes Rivo cough, and the sun is reflecting off the glass, a suffocating glare. Rivo is quiet now and his face seems to have relaxed again. The car is enveloped in silence for a while. The cassette stops, he picks another from the pile. A gospel song.

*Precious Lord, take my hand,*
*Lead me on, let me stand,*
*I am tired, I am weak, I am worn...*

The singer is a Black American man, a descendant of slaves, he's singing his pain, willing hope for a future beyond this earth. On the surface, it has nothing to do with Madagascar, the continents are far apart, but the Presbyterians did come through here. Naivo has known never-ending church services, Sunday school, pastors in black, prayer before meals, just like the singer. He, too, learned detachment, the rigor of Protestant discipline that remains ingrained in the body, the duty to maintain dignity, in spite of it all, with all his strength. He, too, knows the violence of a song that erupts from you when your cooking pot is about to burst. He's about to start singing along, when Rivo says:

"It's funny, there aren't many robins around these days."

Robins? He is certainly mastering the art of throwing his friend off balance.

"Probably pollution."

"The birds are like me, the city has burned them..."

The sentence is said distinctly, crisply.

"And why would it have burned you?"

"Come on, don't be naive."

The city, yes, it had burned them, with its temptations, its excess, that lightheadedness they couldn't handle. The city had been pretty in the beginning, with its laughter, its voices, its illusions of life, of joy, of adventures. It very quickly closed in around them, a dealer of debts, frustration, anger, exhaustion. But the decision had long been settled. They couldn't leave, could never go back to the countryside where they hadn't even had anything to eat. Why tell themselves fantasies?

The road curves, twisting, rocky, climbing the hill. The car lurches, sputtering. The engine strains and Naivo wouldn't have been at all surprised to smell oil or burning rubber, like a tired body's sweat.

"Careful with the car, we're expected in Ambatomanga."

Once again, it sounds like Rivo is answering something, the silence itself.

"By who?"

"That's what they told me last night."

"They who?"

"The dwarves and musicians."

His tone is unquestionable. He'd spoken unhurriedly, yet left no space for Naivo to ask anything. Then he abruptly changes the cassette in the tape player and turns the volume up a notch. Mama Sana's voice fills the car. A full voice, with unending quavers. She sings the South, the Antandroy cowherds calling upon gods, carrying within her the famine, isolation, and suffering of an entire people, south of the South, a people of hunger, and thirst, and distress, a haggard people, dumbstruck, forgotten, hopeless.

"Maty e, kere e," she intones.

"Maty e, maty aho e, I will die, die," Rivo murmurs.

Naivo turns toward him, on the verge of exasperation. Make him be quiet, Rivo's got to be quiet! He's about to scream at him when he sees his friend's hands. He has them folded, as if in prayer, and this young man is shaking.

"Drive slower, you're going too fast, I'm dizzy."

They've gotten a little deeper into the countryside, far from the national routes, approaching the crest of the ridges. It seems as if the plains have dropped away into valleys. If those confined spaces between two hills can be called valleys. The rice fields are even more minuscule, barely visible, hugging every elevation change in the terrain, scraping together every acre of earth. The landscape shows all the signs of some terrible history. The hills are bare. All of the forest that used to cover them had been felled to build houses in the capital, they say, then used for firewood, or it had been burned to make space for zebu pastures, or for no purpose at all, except to express anger, or try to provoke it. More and more rock is being exposed, and in some places, it even looks like the mountain is no more than stone, like all the earth has gone, leaving only the barren kernel of hard, gray rock, its color mimicked in the surroundings. Here, in the nineteenth century, persecuted Christians found shelter in caves, there must have been many of these caves, but they were no longer recorded, no longer known, as the country folk were, little by little, leaving the land to seek shelter in the city.

Naivo doesn't know anymore if this way is pretty or not. It must be pretty, surely, with its tormented lavaka crevasses and its scattered red clay houses. This road, surely it's pretty, but today Rivo is next to him, eyes half-closed and hands folded. And his despair is contagious, making the landscape seem even more harsh and desolate than it is. The eucalyptus beds have been resown, however, they just passed one with stunted trees, and large, fragrant leaves. Naivo, he doesn't really like eucalyptus, he finds it makes the land even more dry, unfit to grow anything else. Easy to see, easy to smell. The earth is becoming hard, brick earth, the color of a blaze. On the edges of big cities, the houses and small rice fields hide the violence done to the land, concrete's prisoner, a land that pollution and exhaust fumes have turned gray or brass. But here in this space, far from cars and traffic, the countryside exposes the whole of it. Every plot reserved for a field is tiny, nothing grows apart from eucalyptus which can survive any wildfire, it's devouring everything. The area has been explored, exploited, then ravaged, a strange space, charred space, memory broken by man's will to burn everything behind him. Here, just two centuries ago, there was an inextricable forest, a small remnant of it can sometimes be seen, down in a valley, or clinging to rocksides, just a few endemic, scrawny, stubborn trees left. Looking at them evokes an image of what all forests must have been like back then, so long ago, centuries ago, an image of a verdant, cool, lush landscape, and undergrowth, and leafy trees, like the ones that are still in Mandraka, a fragrant forest with supple soil, soft underfoot. Now there's nothing left, just gravel and a bit of laterite.

"Drive slower. We might be expected, but we have to take the Queen's road."

"The Queen?"

"Ambohimanambola, Anjiro, Antanamalaza, Ambatomanga, Mantasoa, Moramanga, Anjiro... The town that has money, the town of light, the famous city, the blue rock... The Queen's road that stops in Andevoranto, then in Toamasina, where the boat is waiting to take her to Algeria and then France, the road of the one leaving her country forever."

Naivo allows for silence, to deal with the feeling of suffocation overwhelming him. Rivo's voice is grating on him. He has to make him hush. Stop listening to him talk about disaster.

Talk about poetry or something, and magic, and cities of legend, of joy, no matter what the future holds, a bit of joyful calm, or a dazzling flash, but joy, peace, serenity or something. He's had enough of misfortune, the elegance of despair is only suited to rich people, while his commands him to be handsome, ironic, a player to the bitter end. It's a state of mind, misfortune, a way of seeing things, of seeing yourself in things. There's Rivo, true, the illness, the inevitable, but also this journey, in the shadow of the Queen's. This is the journey they're making, these two who have essentially never seen the sea. They're going there, and in a nice car, the rest can wait. Naivo, he wants happiness, same as his friends, same as other people his age. Eventually he'll find it, and once he does, he'll never let anyone stand in the way of it again. Even Rivo. He agreed to this journey to show him the sea, the waves that crash on the shore, the vast stretches of white sand, and the rhythmic sound of the swells. It's more than desire, it's a dream come true.

He's about to say something sharp when his eyes land on the cheeks of the young man next to him. He can distinctly see the shape of his jawbone, and the skin clinging to the curve of his skull.

"Ambohimanambola, Anjiro, Antanamalaza..."

Rivo drifts between semicoma and lucidity, mumbling, as if talking to himself.

He sings each word, repeating each one several times, his voice quivering, rocking himself like an autistic child, shaken by the wheezing that has returned to punctuate each line. And his words ramble, reel, sometimes rising in a crescendo that collapses in an exhausted breath, in a hiss that ends in that wheezing. It's throbbing, obsessive, enough to scream. Naivo tries to hold it together, clinging to his steering wheel, the winding road, the sound of the engine he monitors, each variation of the landscape, so he doesn't succumb to Rivo's delirium too, or start screaming, or just stop the car and make his friend get out and leave him there on the side of this virtually deserted road and then, finally, breathe, far away from this journey into hell. He's about to stop everything, cut it short, when he hears a voice whispering clearly inside of him:

> *There is a time for misfortune to cease,*
> *A time to break shackles,*
> *A time for peace to finally be.*

The voice is soft, calm, he doesn't even know if it's his own or one restored by his desire, but it hums within him, lulls him, a voice whose words are almost imperceptible, but present deep within him.

And little by little, he feels the peace come. He thinks he can hear the car's engine purring, too. That last thought makes him smile, he's not about to make the car a main character in this story, like the dwarves and other musicians from Rivo's delirium. He's not about to let time be dictated by mechanical temperaments. He's about to tell Rivo that, talk about the purring car, when he sees him smile.

# Jamshid Khan

**Bakhtiyar Ali**

Translated from Kurdish
by Basir Borhani
and Shirzad Alipour

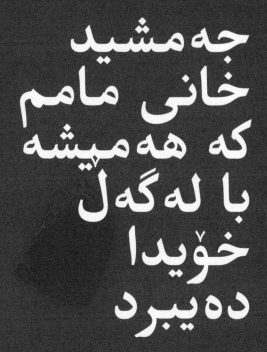

جه‌مشید
خانی مامم
که‌ هه‌میشه‌
با له‌گه‌ل
خۆیدا
ده‌یبرد

ئه‌مجاره‌ مامم زۆر له‌ زه‌وی
به‌رزبووه‌وه‌، پتر له‌ بالای کۆشکێکی
دوو نهۆم له‌سه‌ر سه‌رمان وه‌ک
کۆلاره‌یه‌ک که‌وته‌ مه‌له‌کردن و وه‌ک
بالنده‌یه‌ک له‌ده‌وری نێچیرێک
بسورێته‌وه‌ به‌و چه‌شنه‌ له‌هه‌وادا
ده‌سورا و ده‌چوو...

This time my uncle rose very high
above the ground—higher than
a two-story mansion—and began
to swim in the air above our
heads like a kite, whirling like a
bird circling prey.

IN THE BEGINNING OF 1979, WHEN JAMSHID KHAN WAS ARRES-
ted for the first time, he was seventeen years old. At that time,
the Ba'athists throughout Iraq had started to track, arrest, and
torture communists who had until very recently been among
the principal allies of the revolution and the commander-in-
chief, Saddam Hussein. None of us precisely knows when and
how Jamshid Khan turned into a communist, especially since
there had never before been a communist in our clan. As many
have said, Jamshid endured the suffering of prison with much
resistance and outstanding heroism; his bravery and refusal to
talk were legendary, even among his torturers, who with each
new interrogation resorted to newer and more severe inno-
vations in torment, but to no avail. The Ba'athists transferred
Jamshid Khan in and out of Iraq's infamous and dreadful jails,
and it seems his excessive weight loss and subsequent scrawni-
ness may have originated in the prolonged torment and hunger

he underwent there. Jamshid's former fellow prisoners speak of a sudden, inexplicable weight loss in him at that time. I hardly recollect his appearance before imprisonment; his few photos, from when he was fifteen or sixteen, portray a short, rotund youth who is not all that different from a plump man, well on his way toward obesity. He is not the type of person one would describe as feeble or underweight; instead we see a chubby-cheeked boy whose smiles show signs of a healthy, peaceful childhood. Those who knew him at that age prior to his captivity say that what must have made Jamshid Khan a communist was not his faith in freedom and social justice, but rather his desire for a society in which one could love more easily, in which the relationship between men and women could be less *haram* and therefore less monitored. Whatever the case, Jamshid became extremely thin, losing almost all his weight in prison. The Ba'athists, who placed no value on the lives of men, did not care about his weight loss either. Instead, they deemed it a natural consequence of the efficient, novel methods of torture they had incorporated into their prisons with the aid of experts from abroad.

Nobody knows on precisely what day Jamshid was blown away by the wind. What is known is that his first flight began from a certain prison in Kirkuk, on a cold winter night. That night, an Arab guard had tried to take him to those dreadful interrogators whose relentless coercion, beatings, and threats he had endured for several months. In order to reach the torture chamber from his jail cell, he had to cross a large, open area. During the transfer, something happened which would vividly remain in Jamshid Khan's memory, something he would later relate to all of us with unparalleled pleasure. As he and the guard traversed this open area step-by-step, a commander in a long overcoat, stationed in a room a bit farther back and in need of the bundle of keys in the hands of Jamshid's guard and companion, angrily ordered him to come back and open a door for him. The Arab guard, whom Jamshid later described as "fat, curly-haired, and pimpled," told him, "Wait here and don't move. I'll be back in a moment." Jamshid waited and did not move. Nobody knows the full extent of what happened next, but without question a sudden gust of wind lifted Jamshid Khan off the ground for the first time in his life. Jamshid remembers that in those initial moments he became very dizzy, a tremor of fear sliding through him; he felt himself being blown by the wind, swiftly like a piece of straw. He was lifted higher than the prison walls. First, he was simply pulled up into the sky; when he reached above the rooftops of the Northern Regional Asayish Department—apparently the name of the place where Jamshid had been detained—the wind flattened him horizontally into a recumbent pose, then turned him prostrate with his hands facing southward, playing with him. Still dizzy, Jamshid now had a splitting headache. He did not know what had happened or what was going to happen. He heard shots from below and closed his eyes in fear, as his whole body shook with the terror of a sudden fall which might have torn him to pieces. But the wind carried him farther and farther. Today, Jamshid vaguely remembers that he saw the whole city from the sky. He saw lights, car headlights and the glow from the chain of lamps along the wide streets, but fear did not allow him to look at anything in detail. With a wild gust, the wind swiftly blew him into the depths of the sky, where he passed out in the eternal heights.

No one knows how long Jamshid spent wandering up in the sky or how far he flew. Had the winds and tornados taken him straight to our city—which, of course, was often visited by whirlwinds, storms, and hurricanes from the four corners of the universe—or had the unconscious Khan traveled for quite some time in the sky before falling to the ground? No one knows for sure. What we do know is that one day, after a lengthy flight from the jail, an unconscious Jamshid fell onto the roof of a repair shop and was found by an apprentice in the wee hours of morning.

Jamshid remembers that while he was in the sky he was still a communist, but the very moment he fell onto the roof he was no longer a communist. The wind that carried him from south to north erased his memory of what he had been. The wind continued to blow Jamshid along, and each time his feet touched the ground a drastic change took place in him, and a profound, maniacal obsession pierced through him. After every fall, some portion of his memories was gone and some other portion became clouded. Truth be told, it sometimes seems to me that the effort of writing the life story of this man who never recollects what he is or what he has been is futile.

One late afternoon, Jamshid arrived at Grandfather Hisam Khan's house. Hisam Khan was dumbfounded at the sight of that skeletal, skinny boy, who was nothing but a thin layer of skin dried over a handful of narrow bones. Even so, Jamshid's return after several months of total absence delighted my grandfather. At a time when the Ba'athists' brutality was becoming harsher and harsher, there was little hope that anyone would ever be released from one of their prisons. Those captured by the Ba'athists seldom came out alive, especially if they were communists. At first, Hisam Khan thought the Ba'athists had been unable to prove any accusation against his youngest son and had therefore released him, but when Jamshid said that he had been carried away by the wind, minutely recounting his wanderings up in the air, my grandfather—ever scrupulous and doubtful—was saddened by the realization that his son had either broken out of prison or else lost his mind.

That same day, Jamshid Khan went into hiding for fear of being recaptured by the Ba'athists. And a week later, Uncle Adib Khan's son Smaeel and I became Jamshid's caretakers. Our duty was to keep Jamshid from being blown away by the wind.

Jamshid was only three years older than Smaeel and I, but each of us was several times as burly and heavy as him. When I first saw him again, he was a scraggy, shaky man who bore a striking resemblance to a creature made of straw paper, a thin man who, when viewed from the side, looked like a narrow line, a thread swinging in the air, his body wafting in the breeze. It was our responsibility to bind ourselves to Jamshid Khan on windy days, lest the wind snatch him away. Smaeel and I were cousins and both fifteen years old, but for the past two years we had failed to pass the first year of high school. When our relatives gathered together to resolve Jamshid's situation, we were held in ill repute, considered two unpromising good-for-nothings. Uncle Adib Khan, the oldest son of Hisam Khan, was the first to propose that Smaeel become a lifelong caretaker of his miserable brother. Likewise, my father, Sarfiraz Khan, immediately expressed his fraternity and sympathy by saying that he too would put his son, Salar, at Jamshid's service, since one could not look after or protect him single-handedly.

Smaeel and I were the most useless among our relatives—two youths who were never expected to accomplish anything or have a very bright future. In an effort to avoid being recaptured by the Ba'athists, Jamshid went into hiding from the government and its secret spies, wending his way toward the free mountainous regions until our family could find a better solution for him. Our old village was located in a cold, isolated spot in the mountains. One week after Jamshid's return, my father sat me down in the front seat of his pickup truck and said, "We'll head to Baranok." En route, he told me, "From now on, together with your cousin, Smaeel, you'll be the protectors of your Uncle Jamshid who has escaped from prison. Your uncle will always need you, no matter where he is, and you should never leave him unattended, since he has grown so skinny that the wind could blow him away at any time." I dared neither say nor ask anything at that time, though I understood nothing about my father's final sentence. I had rarely ever spoken with Jamshid Khan. Before his arrest, whenever we visited my grandfather's, my uncle hardly ever came out of his room to greet us; his room on the upper floor of my grandfather's was like a fortified castle, not to be visited by anyone except my uncle and his friends. Jamshid Khan was a college freshman majoring in agriculture when he was arrested. I will admit that I did not like Uncle Jamshid back then, not because he scarcely spoke to us, but rather because he had a particularly aggressive and grave look to him. He always had some pretext for looking down on us disparagingly. Things were, of course, different from his standpoint. At fifteen, when he became a communist, he looked down scornfully and condescendingly on his brothers, his father, Hisam Khan, and his noble relatives, regarding them as vicious, oppressive people. Then he refused to be called Jamshid Khan, insisting we call him *Comrade* Jamshid instead. He also adorned his room with several large photographs of Marx and Engels. On that day when I went with my father to our ancient village, Baranok, I still held that old image of Jamshid in my mind—the image of a communist who looked down contemptuously on us noblemen. By the time our car got there, Smaeel and Uncle Adib Khan had already arrived. Jamshid was sitting in the middle of a big room on a colorful Persian carpet beside Grandfather Hisam. At that point, I had not set eyes upon Jamshid Khan for a year and a half. Physically, he was nothing like the Jamshid of former days. What really piqued Smaeel's and my interest was that, although extreme torment had completely whittled Uncle Jamshid's body away, it had had no effect on his pride or self-esteem. Imprisonment had not only failed to destroy Jamshid, it had inflated him. Hisam Khan, whom we called the Grand Khan, turned to Smaeel and me and said, "The Ba'athists have tortured Jamshid so badly that he has no weight left to him. My son is melting into a soul without a body. You shouldn't leave him on his own until he regains some weight and is able to lay heavy steps on the ground again. Fasten him to yourselves whenever he goes out and don't let go of him on stormy days. You'd better not take him out on such days. You're also responsible for keeping an eye on Jamshid's nutrition and health. Tomorrow we'll fetch Doctor Najib Khan to meticulously examine him. And you, Jamshid, should listen to whatever Doctor Najib says or tells you to eat. I have asked Saleh Hindi's household here to bake you bread daily. And you two must under no condition take Jamshid close to where the Iraqi Army has camped. We should wait for amnesty from the government to pave the way for his return to the city; until then, whatever happens, you mustn't neglect Uncle Jamshid."

This was an easy, pleasant task for Cousin Smaeel, who had his heart set on learning languages, sitting around, and studying. Both Smaeel and I detested school. But Smaeel yearned for a sedentary lifestyle and a world of books, unlike me who wished to squander my time wandering aimlessly, goofing off, and flirting with women. That first day, Hisam Khan showed us several pieces of short, thick ropes and said, "Whenever you go out together, you should walk beside Uncle Jamshid and both—or at least one of you—keep a firm hold on the rope tied around his waist. If need be, one of you should wrap the other end of the rope around yourself lest the wind easily whisk my son away. If the wind is very strong, both of you should grasp the rope so he is fixed firmly to the ground, since if the wind blows him away again, God only knows what will become of him or where he will drop down."

At first, Jamshid remained silent, but later he looked at us like someone who pokes fun at everything and shook his head, repeating some of my grandfather's sentences and words.

As that evening came to an end, my father, Sarfiraz Khan, and Smaeel's father, Adib Khan, left us with two bits of advice: They reminded us not to forget how much Jamshid meant to them, and then they warned us that, if something happened to him, Hisam Khan would most definitely disinherit us, denying us land and patrimony. Later, when Smaeel and I were left to ourselves, Smaeel said he thought this task would be far more pleasurable than school, since out here we would be able to learn things while surrounded by nature. I agreed with him, but it had been difficult for me to leave the city since it meant no longer getting to see any of the girls I knew there. Additionally, over the past two years, I had regularly snuck out to the movie theater unbeknownst to my father or any of my relatives, and watching Indian films had become a significant part of my life. Now, I had to put everything aside and devote myself wholeheartedly to serving someone I did not even like. To me, this was neither a pleasant nor worthwhile adventure.

Our initial meeting with Jamshid Khan did not turn out to be so exceptional. All I could do was look at his thin, scraggy body in dismay. Jamshid talked a little about his imprisonment. He told us that he had suffered greatly under torture but claimed that no one in this world could wrest anything from him by force. In the middle of the conversation, a special tailor arrived to make him clothes suited to his unique physical form. From that day forward until our return to the city, Uncle Jamshid—apart from us who were his constant protectors—had a special doctor and tailor at his service. With the tone of someone who alone knows his own wants, Jamshid told us we must do whatever he wanted, get him everything he craved, and keep his secrets safe. At the time, I thought that Jamshid intended to further his communist causes without my grandfather's knowledge; later I realized that not only did he no longer cherish such ideas, but he felt great scorn for the communists of the world.

Baranok itself was a small village with no more than ten families. That first evening, Smaeel and I wrapped the rope around Jamshid's body, Smaeel gripping the end of a remaining line, and took him to the hamlet mosque to fetch water. I could tell Jamshid longed to walk around the village and see the world again. He had harbored a strong desire to see and experience nature ever since his farewell to communism. On that evening, a soft breeze was wafting, but it lacked enough force to lift him up into the air. All the villagers old and young had come out to see this small, skinny man, and he was delightfully taking the lead. The few old people who lived in the village and could remember the birth of Jamshid's father welcomed him, and then inquired about the secret behind the rope, one of the ends of which was always in Smaeel's or my hands. Jamshid haughtily replied, "This rope is helpful on stormy days, preventing Your Majesty from being carried away if a strong whirlwind begins to blow."

During that time, Jamshid did not wish to associate with simple, ordinary people; for this reason, that night he forced us to venture outside the village, leading us up a small mountain under the glint of moonlight until we stopped on top of a small hill. From that night onward, I felt Jamshid longed to fly. As he stood up on that hill, I could tell he was eagerly expecting the wind, but nothing blew except a very gentle breeze. Jamshid kept us there until late at night without saying anything specific. He just stood there inhaling clean air, watching the stars, and thinking of something totally unknown to us.

The next day, when Doctor Najib came and examined Khan, he was awestruck, like someone beholding a great miracle.

Afterward, the doctor pulled us aside and warned us to watch him carefully since, he believed, Khan would likely be seized by sudden fits of aggression or else sink into periods of depression and possibly even try to commit suicide. The doctor said Jamshid's true weight resided only in his head, and what was left to his body was so scanty and insignificant that it lay beyond the realm of medical research and scientific reasoning. He also suggested Jamshid eat foods high in fat and move about sparingly for a while to see if it was possible for him to regain his strength. With the passage of time, the verity and veracity of much of what Doctor Najib said was realized, but in all that time I was with Jamshid, his overeating and merrymaking did nothing to regain his weight or rectify his situation.

After Doctor Najib's departure that day, Jamshid—speaking disparagingly of the doctor—told us that he never intended to regain his weight because he did not wish to be stuck to the ground forever. Jamshid never took the medicine the doctor prescribed for him; instead, he threw the pills into the sewer whenever he happened to go to the village mosque. The day we discovered this, he became suddenly cruel and aggressive, commanding us not to tell anyone of his utter disregard for the doctor's advice, especially not Grandfather Hisam.

From the very first day, Smaeel and I were scared of him. Even though we were much stronger and sturdier, he could force us into doing anything he wished simply with a look. Early on, he had told us, "If we're *good to each other*, we'll have a long life ahead of us together."

At first, I did not believe that the wind could actually blow Jamshid into the air. I told Smaeel it was all a big lie, a fabricated story to oust us from our city. I said the Khans must have held a clandestine meeting and decided to hide us from public scrutiny, since our repeated failures at school had risked the good name and reputation of our family, dishonoring our clan. Smaeel said that no secret meeting had occurred, that we had been assigned this important yet easy task simply because the two of us were the most useless good-for-nothings in our clan. Afterward, he looked at me woefully and said, "I don't mind busying myself to my last breath with this half-human who doesn't ask us for anything but to hold him by a rope, even though I don't have a good feeling about it and fear that one day a disaster will befall us for what we're doing." Contrary to Smaeel's view, which was simultaneously simplistic and tragic, I was confident our task was no easy one and would prove to be challenging in the future, though at that time I did not know what problems were in store, or how they would turn out.

During our first week in Baranok the wind did not blow at all. The air was so still that Jamshid did not let us bind him with rope. He led the way and rambled among the fields, farms, rivers, and surrounding grove of sycamores. I came to know my uncle then as a devoted lover of flowers, fruits, and trees. Though he did not place much value in a man's life, he loved to ramble and amble out in nature with a passion. Finally, at the end of the second week, the trees started to shake, signaling the arrival of a strong wind. One night when the wind was very intense, Jamshid told us to tie together whatever ropes we possessed and take him out. Smaeel and I were scared at first and did not want to listen to him because the storm was getting more and more violent, but once the world turned completely dark and the people of Baranok had fallen asleep, he forced us. Finding ourselves with no other choice, we bound him to ourselves with ropes, packed all the other ropes into a ragged sack, took his hands, and followed him out.

This was his first exposure to wind since his release from the Ba'athists' prison.

Smaeel and I each carried a handheld flashlight, which we lit in turn. We walked through the thick of night to the top of those knolls where we had crossed paths quite often in the happy days of our youth. The wind was so fierce there that it almost carried us off. We both held Jamshid tightly so the wind would not blow him away. When we got to the top, Jamshid said, "Stay where you are and let go of me." At first, we did not want to let him go, but he comforted us, saying, "Don't be frightened. Can't you see I am tied to your waists with two thick cords, so that even if the wind takes me away, you can bring me back?" We loosened our grip on the ropes and saw for the first time how the wind could pick someone up off the earth. In the twinkling of an eye, Jamshid was a weightless creature in the air once again. Since the ropes were short, he did not stand a chance of getting very far from us or of soaring too high above the earth. He ordered us from above to bring him down and tie all the ropes we had brought into one long piece, wrapping one end around his waist and the other around our hands. While Smaeel held Jamshid Khan tightly, I took all the ropes out, tied them firmly together, and fastened them solidly around his waist. Then, with the help of Smaeel, I gradually released Jamshid to the wind. This time my uncle rose very high above the ground—higher than a two-story mansion—and began to swim in the air above our heads like a kite, whirling like a bird circling prey. This was when I came to believe that Jamshid reveled so much in flying that he would never give it up and our lives would forever be bound to his desire to watch the world from above. From up in the sky, Jamshid began to speak. He told us he was feeling something that he had never experienced before in his life, a feeling far beyond the ecstasy of someone who flew in the wind and could look downward from above; rather it was the feeling of someone who knew he had a life no one else could experience, who did things no one else could do and saw things no one else could see. That night was so dark that neither we, standing on the hillock, nor Jamshid, high up in the sky, could see much of anything, but Jamshid enjoyed this total darkness. Since that night, Jamshid Khan strove to acclimate himself to the movements of the wind, getting used to turning, moving, and steering his body without letting the rope twist or cause him discomfort.

Upon returning home that night, Jamshid Khan was ecstatic. He was certain that his flight from prison would not be his only flight, that he would have the opportunity to fly and live like a bird his whole life. I believe that same night he came to the realization that he would be in dire need of us, grasping that from then on his life depended on the rope Smaeel and I controlled from the ground. After that flight, his behavior toward us changed; he began to treat us in the friendliest possible manner.

During the following days, the storm continued blowing through Baranok and its surrounding regions. Jamshid Khan said, "This windstorm is a good opportunity to practice because I must learn two important things: one is how to fly in the wind and the other is how to walk on the ground. My ability to walk normally on the ground is just as important as my ability to fly in the sky, since it would be a huge disgrace to me and all our clan's noblemen if someday the wind blew me about in public."

The main problem in the beginning was the quality and type of ropes. The ropes we were supposed to use in the daytime among other people were very short ones, binding Jamshid Khan to us in such a way that sometimes we had to walk like conjoined triplets so that people did not notice the ropes between us, yet at the same time ensuring that a sudden wind would not whisk him away.

We began to spend every windy day developing these defensive tactics, practicing walking in an unobtrusive manner. Jamshid had someone bring us all kinds and colors of rope from the city, and Iran as well. During this time, testing the strength and flexibility of the ropes and noting their various colors had become an important part of our life. Jamshid himself chose the color and thickness of the ropes before every outing, and we always made sure to have some auxiliary ones, which I carried in a black sack in case they were needed. At the same time, Smaeel had his own desires and dreams. He spent his free time studying Arabic and English. Jamshid also had someone bring him books from the city, one of which was Charles Darwin's *The Origin of Species*. The few months we spent in Baranok, my uncle devoted his time fully to the perusal of this book because, while he was flying, it had occurred to him to present a counter-theory proving that humans had evolved from birds and not from apes. Smaeel and I spent several nights excavating some ancient graves by stealth in the Baranok cemetery, exhuming their bones so that Jamshid could compare them with the bird bones left on the *sofreh* cloth after lunch. During that same period, he began corresponding with some biology teachers in the city, and from there, he found the addresses of several university professors in Baghdad who were specialists in the theory of evolution. This correspondence proved disappointing for my uncle: all the professors and teachers unanimously agreed that such a standpoint was wildly inaccurate, nothing beyond the hallucinations of a lunatic. Jamshid's theory was predicated on three principles, and Smaeel and he spent a majority of their time pondering and discussing these three principles. Jamshid's first principle was that man's conception of God as a creature that looks down on human beings from above had its roots in human archetypes, that is to say, back when man could fly. He believed the God of the heavens was nothing but man's memory of his heavenly, winged ancestors. The second principle, which Jamshid said he had drawn from Darwin's theories, was that, if survival was only for the fittest and the strongest, then humankind could never have survived against the fierce and powerful beasts of nature—compared to which he had never been the fittest and the strongest—without possessing wings. His third principle was that he himself was proof that man had originally possessed wings.

Though my uncle's theory was extremely weak and, as Smaeel put it, had not managed to discover a common morphological lineage between men and birds, it had become an all-consuming obsession for him during the time we spent in Baranok. He continuously complained that he did not know English and therefore could not penetrate the surface of the theory, for he believed that in today's world any text written in non-European languages was of little value. Every day he repeated that our oriental languages were not the languages of science, but rather the languages of riding camels and raising mules.

Try as he might, Jamshid Khan never managed to bring his theory to full fruition, but as time passed, he became more and more adept at flying. And we became experienced in moving, loosening, and pulling the ropes. One night, by chaining the ropes together, Jamshid rose about one hundred meters up into the sky, and the higher he flew, the less he weighed and the easier it was for us to hold him. At first, I thought my uncle would perhaps lose his nerve and stop at a certain height, but the higher he ascended, the more pleasure he found in flying, the more love he felt toward the wind, and the more his sense of uniqueness grew. One night, when Grandfather Hisam, my father, and Uncle Adib came from the city exclusively to pay us a visit, they accompanied us and saw Jamshid fly with their own eyes. I noticed both happiness and sadness on my grandfather's face; on the one hand, my grandfather liked the fact that his son could fly, but he was also afraid that this ability might ruin everything, forever preventing him from living a normal life. Uncle Adib was the first to insist that Jamshid never fly in daylight, since a flying Khan was likely to be the butt of jokes and mockery or else a source of fear and terror for the public, potentially leading to civil disturbance and incurable moral problems. Uncle Adib said, "People have wives and children and don't want to be watched from above." Soon, Hisam Khan too came to agree with my uncle's opinion that Smaeel and I must never fly Jamshid in daylight, for this would be a grave mistake. Jamshid easily gave in to the decision before my grandfather, promising he would not force us to take him flying during the daytime.

In 1980, the Ba'athists granted amnesty to all those who had been accused of political crimes. One day, Hisam Khan and my father arrived together and spent a great deal of time conversing with Jamshid alone. They had rarely held such secret, private conversations before. After several hours, Jamshid emerged with a disappointed and rather sad countenance. Jamshid was, of course, not the type of person who could stay in the same place for too long. Though we had had no problems in Baranok and had spent the last few months peacefully and comfortably, Khan was gradually getting bored with everything. Obviously, it would have been unreasonable to live the rest of our lives in that backwater hamlet. But when Grandfather Hisam said that the government's amnesty would soon come to include Jamshid Khan and that he would then have to surrender himself, Smaeel and I did not feel as though our prayers had been answered by this news. Rather we felt heavy with dismay and doubt. Life with Jamshid Khan was easier in this remote village than it would be in the city. I pictured the three of us bound together, walking the city streets and rambling around hand in hand year-round, and feared this would make people talk or make fun of us. But nobody paid heed to my fears. Grandfather Hisam Khan and Grandmother Piroz Khan did not wish for their son to be a fugitive in the mountains any longer; besides, many of our noble relatives did not want to get into trouble with the government because of Jamshid.

One morning, after we had spent several months together, our relative Davood Khan—whom we all knew to be in close contact with officials of the Ba'athist Party—turned up in Baranok and, along with my grandfather, took Jamshid to register his name for amnesty. Later that same afternoon, a vehicle drove Smaeel and me back to the city.

Arriving at my grandfather's door, I realized I had become so estranged that it was as though I had been out in the wilderness for many years and was now frightened by the atmosphere and incandescence of the city. As I got out of the car and moved toward Hisam Khan's upstairs room, I knew I was not in the slightest degree similar to the boy that had once left the city. I felt that what had passed was permanently past and what was gone was gone forever.

# Place Memory

**Dorota Brauntsch**

Translated from Polish
by Sean Gasper Bye

# Pamięć
# miejsca

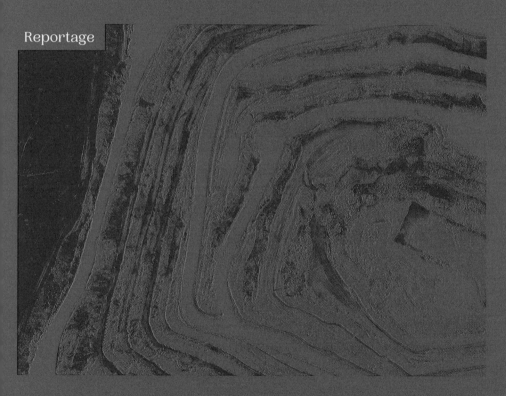

And that's what he fears most. New owners will come and cut down, erase, demolish. Everything down to zero. As if none of this had ever existed.

I tego boi się najbardziej. Przyjdą nowi właściciele i wytną, wykasują, zburzą. Wszystko do zera. Jak gdyby tamtych nigdy nie było.

THE BRANCHES TUMBLE DOWN LIKE CLUMPS OF SNIPPED-OFF hair at the barbershop, like locks of curls, and settle into odd patterns on the ground. Softly and silently, because the triple-insulated window muffles the dull thumps on the frozen ground. When Szymon was small, he would press his palms against the cool pane to get close, as close as possible to the old apple trees hunched toward the ground, the dignified horse chestnuts that stretched along the road, the lindens growing near the farms. "You're leaving fingerprints"—his mother's reproachful voice would say, pulling him out of his reverie.

*

The terrain here undulates steeply. Hills rise and fall, suddenly obscuring the vista, only to reveal a moment later the green, brown, and russet lines of fields, stretching to the sky. You can meander among the rises like this on a bike, playing hide-and-seek with the horizon. The Vistula River once flowed near here, but during the spring melt the waters never reached the homesteads built on higher ground. That's why this was a good place to settle. And also because when the river waters fell back, the ground was fertile; the meadows turned white in May, yellow in June, and pink in August. The people grazed cattle, picked clover, mowed grass, dried hay.

The first written mention of the homesteader from Łąka named Jan Krucek, also known as Chorzus, dates from 1586. The last of the Chorzus line, Wawrzyniec, died 273 years later. His widow, Anna, took a new husband—Josef Jazowy, who in 1861 replaced the old wooden cottage the Chorzuses had built long ago with a brick masonry building. Paweł—Szymon's great-grandfather—was born in 1876, and his grandmother Helena in the generation after that. Szymon's mother, Monika, came into the world one hundred and fifty years after Wawrzyniec's death, but people in the village still called her "Old Lady Korzus" (Korzus from Chorzus), even though not a drop of Chorzus family blood flowed in her veins.

Szymon says: That was place memory, the law of the land here.

\*

A cow's tongue is coarse and hard.

Steamed potatoes mixed with grain mash tastes like fresh earth.

Hay is prickly.

Sleeping on hay is overrated.

Never go up to a horse from behind.

Mown grass is moist and gently warm.

The gunk in the cowshed sticks to your feet.

Geese nip your calves.

Old quilts are heavy and cold.

You're not allowed to name little piglets.

Kary the Horse was king.

\*

It's hard to keep all the memories of that house straight in his head. A whirl of smells, sounds, and tastes. The life of the old brick cottage was above all a life with animals. Kary the Horse was lord and master on the farm. Grandpa kept saying he was king of the animals. There was only one rule: you could go up to a horse, you could pet its forehead or muzzle, but you could never, ever, come up to it from behind—Grandpa dealt out harsh punishments for that. There were Mela and Baśka the cows, and their little bullocks. You could feed the cows hay—they had coarse and hard tongues. Grandma milked them every evening, and the children couldn't believe how much milk there was inside one cow. Early in the morning, Grandma would make butter, quark, cream, and *kiszka*— meaning soured milk, which in summer she served with fried potatoes over pork cracklings for lunch. The only better thing to eat were the steamed potatoes and so-called grain mash that got cooked for the pigs.

An unwritten hierarchy prevailed. The animals were divided into those with names and those without. Szymon couldn't understand why he wasn't allowed to name the little piglets.

And then one year—he was seven or eight—he attended a pig slaughter. The village butcher called him into the kitchen. High on a hook that usually held up a swing, there hung a pig. The butcher told him to hold out his hands and placed the scooped-out entrails into the boy's arms. It scared the life out of Szymon. He never thought again about giving names to the little piglets.

*

Who in the village doesn't remember good old Rudolf? Everyone could hear him when he was on his way back from drinking at the Goldfish. He would shout at the authorities in

Polish, at his neighbors in German, at his family in Silesian. Once he very nearly drowned a stubborn communist policeman in a pig trough. Another time he smashed up a propaganda loudspeaker because he didn't like its new vision for the village. He brewed moonshine, poached, smoked meat; to him, the greatest delicacy was scrambled eggs with pig brains. He hated hot food. He didn't have time to wait for it to cool down. He'd pour cold water into soup, because there was work waiting for him. "Well, Ah cain't cook it cold," his exasperated wife would say. Sometimes he'd sit by the well and weave wicker baskets, bind up brooms, play the harmonica. Sometimes he'd let you pet his horse.

Grandpa Rudolf—stern and good. Fire and water. Moonshine and buttermilk.

In the 1980s, Szymon's parents built themselves a house across from his grandparents' farm. The narrow road they lived on was like Toffler's "leading edge": on one side, old homesteads—on the other, new colors, shapes, and materials. Just cross the road, step through the wooden gate, and you'd fall into a time warp.

"I got to experience the last stage of the house's life," says Szymon, who started collecting old objects no one had any use for way back when his father was still alive. A lamp, turn-of-the-century glass medicine bottles, tools; then documents, photos, and finally stories. He worked out his family's history, using a special computer program to arrange it on a family tree.

Szymon looks out the windows of his parents' house at his grandparents' cottage, which for months has been standing empty. The whole family dreams that someone will buy this brick dwelling and move in. But it's well known these traditional cottages are nothing but trouble. An old house lowers the value of a property. You're better off demolishing it right away and—as the real estate experts put it—setting the lot under the structure free.

Everyone in the area is setting free.

It's worse when the building is on the historic register. No one will buy one of these properties with a crumbling cottage on it. You can't demolish it; you have to wait until it falls down on its own. But there are some who've sniffed out a decent business from all this. They buy a so-called "deep freezer"—a lot with a building on the historic register—for pennies. And then they wait patiently, sometimes years on end, for the elements to take their toll. They might also lend a little hand to the ravages of time: make a hole in the roof, attract a lightning bolt... Once the building is in danger of collapse, the conservator will let you tear it down, since human safety is the most important thing. And that's when the financial investment "thaws"—the property you bought for pennies, liberated from its brickwork ruin, gains value. If Szymon won the lottery he'd buy up this whole little corner of the world, because his grandparents' house neighbors on another old house from the mid-nineteenth century. That one was put up for sale not long ago, and part of the ancient forest that grew around it has recently been cut down.

The fathers, as they call them in the countryside, have died off one by one, and their houses are departing with them. The rural landscape is also vanishing.

To Szymon, these houses only make sense as part of a whole—with the old orchard, the old garden, the old well, and the centenarian trees around the barn. They are a unity. Indivisible, complete. A little universe.

"Or is the point maybe that people don't want these histories at all? This past?" he wonders. "Would they rather reset everything to zero and start their own history from scratch?"

And that's what he fears most. New owners will come and cut down, erase, demolish. Everything down to zero.

As if none of this had ever existed.

In the eighties there were no streetlights in this part of the village. Szymon liked to watch the shadows gathering around his grandparents' cottage, light suddenly flaring up in the darkness. The sight of illuminated panes in lattice windows used to soothe him. Now he doesn't even glance out there in the evening, because why would he? He knows he'll see nothing but black night.

*

Last fall the wind blew down an old apple tree. Szymon cut off a branch and tried to root it, but it didn't take. He wanted to save it because the apple tree came from somewhere that no longer exists. Or rather, it does exist, just at the bottom of a lake: in a part of the village flooded by the accumulated waters behind a dam.

In the 1950s, a major investment of the six-year plan was built—the Goczałkowice Reservoir. It was meant to supply drinking water to the local residents, as well as industrial water to the Upper Silesian Industrial Region (USIR). While the reservoir was being built, a spring that until then had fed the wells in Łąka changed course and started emptying into the enormous belly of the lake. Some wells went totally dry; in others, the water took on a rusty color or was so low it could no longer be drawn. While the waterworks quickly started delivering water to the USIR, it only made it to Łąka thirty years later.

Many farms ended up beneath the waters of Goczałkowice Reservoir, including the house where Szymon's grandfather had lived before he married Helena and moved into the Chorzus family home.

The displaced villagers had little time, some only a few days, to vacate their dwellings. Then they had to move from relative to relative, staying in the cellars of newly built houses or in barns. Many from that part of the village received lots in a new development of small single-family homes in Pszczyna. To this day, the locals call them *utopcy*—ghosts of the drowned.

One of the last things his grandfather managed to take with him was the branch of an apple tree that grew near the stoop of their family home. He grafted it in the orchard of the Chorzuses' farm. That's why Szymon finds it so hard to let go of this fallen apple tree.

"I wanted something to last from that house, from my great-grandparents' land that disappeared underwater. Besides, I think it's really important to preserve old varieties of apple trees. Because those are disappearing too. There used to be hundreds of types of apple trees in the Polish country-side, now in the commercial orchards they grow barely a few different species."

*

A cow's tongue is coarse and hard.

Steamed potatoes mixed with grain mash tastes like fresh earth.

Hay is prickly.
Sleeping on hay is overrated.
Never go up to a horse from behind.
Mown grass is moist and gently warm.
The gunk in the cowshed sticks to your feet.
Geese nip your calves.
Old quilts are heavy and cold.
You're not allowed to name little piglets.
Kary the Horse was king.

*

On that day he was awakened by the roar of chainsaws. He pushed the bedroom window shut and ran into the living room. He pressed his face to the windowpane. The trees had stood there forever and they were meant to keep going on, like a straight line with no beginning or end. And suddenly someone had started chopping that continuousness into pieces.

Now Szymon understood this view had never belonged to him.

# The Weather Woman

**Tamar Weiss-Gabbay**

Translated from Hebrew by
Jessica Cohen

# החזאית

When she was a child she thought she
loved these forces of nature, that she
and they were on the same side,
supporting each other. She assumed
they were her home, in this town
and its untamed surroundings.
That she knew them, and they her.

בילדותה חשבה שהיא אוהבת את
איתני הטבע הללו, שהיא והם באותו
צד, זה בעד זה. הניחה שהם הבית
שלה, בעיירה הזו וסביבותיה הפראיות.
שהיא מכירה אותם, והם אותה.

SHE AMBLED ONTO THE MAIN STREET OF HER TOWN LIKE A lone rider who has dismounted his horse to survey the surroundings. Her perpetual beige corduroy overalls were slightly faded but clean, as was the white T-shirt she wore underneath. Tied loosely around her waist was a blue plaid shirt, and she held a straw hat. She started walking down the street. A mournful harmonica played somewhere in the distance (and if it didn't, it should have). Tumbleweed probably blew past her in the wind and vanished onto the horizon. Several pairs of eyes ought to have been watching her through slits in the houses' blinds, admiringly yet anxiously following the woman who walked slowly, alone at midday on the silent street, like a gunslinger to a duel.

As she walked, her braided gray-black hair hardly moved on her shoulder.

She was not heading to a duel. She would walk only as far

as the cliffs on the edge of town. She might be able to glance down and see, or at least hear, if they really had descended into the deep marlstone canyon to silence the bothersome howling.

She would just look. Just check. You might think that, as the lone rider, she would intervene and see justice done. That, after all, was what she had done since returning to this place three decades ago, as a pensive but vibrant young twenty-three-year-old who popped up in town one day, rented a small apartment, and set up her station on the rooftop. She spent weeks developing it, ordering and installing equipment, and when she inaugurated it, she was a heroine taking the law into her own hands, imposing order to benefit a community that had trouble caring for itself. In a different sort of place, they would have cheered her on and doted on her, but here, in her hometown, they sufficed with deep nods of appreciation and a firm handshake. Every time she walked down the main street they were there.

Her weather station was the first to encompass an area that not a single other forecast paid any attention to, a region whose conditions differed from those around it. On that clifftop, over-looking the small but deep canyon, she did more than address the dilemma of whether or not to take a sweater. Her independent enterprise, which embodied social contribution and was the product of intelligent planning, enabled her to interpret the ramifications of low-pressure systems and variances on local temperatures, and most importantly, to understand when rain and wind in the eastern mountains would result in floods in the town's vicinity. She could calculate when the runoff would flow down the other side of the mountains, sparing the town and the small canyon, and when its route would cover the town-side of the incline and send its fat worms crawling, digging, squirming, until they emerged like fingers from a giant hand that rakes up everything in its path and hurls it into the ravine. The locals had good reason for referring to this type of flood as "the beast." Past floods had caused severe property damage, one fatality from a fallen tree, serious injuries sustained by two girls in two separate floods, and several pets swept away in the current, including her own dog.

She'd lost the dog when she was already forecasting the weather and knew a flood was coming, yet she'd accidentally left him outside. He was a shepherd mix who needed more exercise than she had the strength for, so she sometimes let him roam free. This was acceptable: dogs who were strictly trained not to soil, bark at passersby, or growl were allowed to wander the streets. They would come home when whistled for. When her dog scratched at the door, she would let him in and say, "Hi," and he would come over to be petted and then drink from his water bowl. He had a good life with her. After the flood she couldn't find him. She covered the whole town, whistling for him. Days went by but he didn't come home.

Other than that loss, however, resulting from her own grave mistake, there were no disasters in all her years of forecasting. There was no doubt: she was the hometown hero who'd come back to save it. Her forecasts could be trusted. The townsfolk awaited her predictions and took heed of them, unlike when Noah had warned of the flood. Children and dogs were called home, sandbags were stacked. A true prophet is recognized by the validity of his predictions. They were her believers.

The earth turned slightly on its axis, positioning the sun in the center of the sky above the walking woman. The houses' shadows grew smaller. She put her hat on.

If there were furtive glances following her, she was used to that. Glances were always there, even if they'd changed over the years. And perhaps they hadn't changed and it was only her imagination. Her forecasts, after all, were just as accurate as they'd always been. The methods had evolved and grown more sophisticated, because she made a point of staying current: she now used radar data, and her hydrological model calculated the current in the drainage basin and could be applied either deterministically—would there be a flood or wouldn't there?—or in a way that accounted for random factors and presented probabilities. She phrased the forecast in simple, lucid language, authoritative but frank when it came to misgivings, scenarios, and odds. She chose her words thoughtfully. Sometimes she slipped in an inside joke: High winds are coming—let's hope Brown's awning doesn't fly off on its travels again! They loved it. The weather forecast was their shared destiny.

"He said we're going hiking this weekend," said her niece a week ago, while the two of them sat on the porch eating dinner. "He" was the man who oversaw the cadre of volunteers, which included her niece. She knew him. He was from her parents' generation and had been somewhat friendly with them. He had green eyes that he always narrowed into slits, but they still projected a serious, wise hue, with the crow's-feet around them adding charm. Whenever he used to run into her parents, he would always explain something to them in an enthusiastic and well-meaning voice. As a girl, she'd secretly referred to him as "Green Eyes." In the early days of her weather station, when they'd met one day by chance, a spark of green flew out of his eyes into her brown ones, and he shook her hand vehemently and pressed down on her shoulder with his other hand. "That's the idea. We'll put up a fight, and together we'll win in this place," he said.

Her niece, now eighteen, was visiting for her fourth summer in a row. A nature-lover who liked agricultural work, she was spending two months volunteering in the vineyards. Green Eyes assigned the volunteers their shifts and inspired them with talk of how important the work was. He also organized cultural activities, movies, lectures, and hikes. Her niece joined in, made local friends, and basked in the aura of her aunt, whom she had admired since she was a girl, an occasional visitor who saw everything. They always ate dinner on the porch together during the summers, hidden from view by the vine leaves and the clusters of grapes. Now fall was coming and the porch was exposed. Her niece was planning to stay until September, when her studies would begin.

"Will it rain this weekend?" she asked her aunt, prodding her stir-fry with a fork. "We need to know because we might hike down into the canyon."

They'd never talked very much. At first because they hadn't wanted to burden each other while living together, and later because they'd cultivated an illusion of understanding beyond words. They engaged only in short conversations about the day's schedule, plans, changes. Neither wanted to say anything of substance, fearing this might introduce complications and distance between them, nor say anything too trivial, too foolish, and disappoint the admirer or the object of admiration. And so this year, when the niece had arrived at the beginning of summer vacation and asked about the dog, of whom she was very fond, her aunt did not tell her about how she'd failed to call him back to the ark in time. All she said, after some thought, and very deliberately, was: He's not with us anymore.

The niece would have surely been surprised to discover that her venerated aunt cared what she thought about her. That she considered her words, that she was in any way vulnerable. Then again, perhaps she would no longer have been all that surprised. Last summer something in her young, impressionable tone of voice and her admiring look had vanished. But that was fine— she was growing up. And perhaps she'd heard people saying things.

What things? She continued to walk down the street, thrusting her hands deep into her overall pockets. In the early years they'd seen her as a savior. A cowgirl who'd lassoed and tied down the unruly weather. Had she bent it to her will? Some thought she was even capable of that. Of course they didn't exactly believe it, but they joked about putting in requests for certain kinds of weather. When Green Eyes ran into her, he would quip good-naturedly: How much do you charge for three days of showers in the north orchard? Is there a friends and family discount? Put in a good word for us.

She answered everyone with a blank face: I'll do my best.

She did not talk much with the four-thousand residents of her town either. She knew they would want to discuss the weather, which for them was usually a topic of small talk, while for her—

What was it for her?

But it wasn't just small talk. They were afraid of a flood. They depended on her, and it was her job to protect them. Or so they thought. She tried to remember how she herself had perceived her job back then. Until not long ago. Until early spring.

Because in early spring they'd finally built the pipeline, the underground duct that collected the floodwaters into its wide mouth, trapped the frothing spate inside sealed concrete, and led it, like an excitable puppy on a leash, beneath the town to the deep canyon, where it set the torrent free to roil between the walls of rock, onward and downward, until it calmed, until it died.

And once the concrete pipeline was built, a different tone had entered their conversations with and about her.

Or perhaps that tone had always been there and she hadn't noticed? Had they felt so dependent and grateful that they'd never dared to feel any of these things, much less express them? Now they gave free rein to their expectations of her— and to their disappointments. After an undesirable forecast, for a heat wave or haze, they avoided her eyes when they came across her in the street, and the curl of their lips could not hide a touch of childish anger. As if she could have forecasted differently, prophesied something more pleasant, made adaptions. If she'd only wanted to. They did not say this explicitly, nor did they really think it—that would have been absurd! Completely illogical. But before a hoped-for rain shower or a weekend with outdoor plans, if they met her just as she was about to release the forecast, they looked at her imploringly: Adjust the weather. If you must—lie to us.

Professional as always and faithful to herself, she of course made a point of upholding accuracy.

As she had done last winter, throughout the debates over the construction of the pipeline.

That was when talk of the climate crisis first trickled into town, and it continued to slither in, at first only in softly spoken ripples. There were those who murmured that even a giant pipeline would not suffice, that within a few years it would not be able to contain the massive floods. And what if after years of floods, the cliff eroded to the point of crumbling and the town itself collapsed into the canyon? Perhaps it was best to mobilize ahead of time, to seek compensation and leave. But they were a quiet minority. To the majority it was clear: They'd invested everything in this place. They'd overcome obstacles, converted challenges into opportunities. Here the sun ripened the grapes early, the dry winds kept pests away, the town was flourishing, expanding. Blocked on three sides by the mountains, canyon, and vineyards, it was spreading south into the scrubland, considerately leaving an enclave for the local gazelle population. Using wisdom and initiative, they had created a paradise in this place. Comfortable houses, wooden decks, yards, and so much nature everywhere. And so most of them supported the pipeline. It would solve the problem once and for all.

At first, she did not voice an opinion because pipes and drainage were not her expertise. But she soon felt that she was expected to make her position known, to lend support. Or even to object—anything but stay quiet. Her silence troubled them, they found it suspicious.

But what was there to suspect?

Perhaps they felt that if she was neither for nor against it, that meant she didn't care. Perhaps she no longer had any solidarity, perhaps she was no longer one of them, perhaps she'd crossed over—but to whose side?

She began to suspect herself. Maybe she really had grown apart from them. She used to feel a sense of belonging, that she was working for them. Maybe she could work harder, give them something better.

In those days, when residents saw her on the street, whether they supported the pipeline or not, they would give her little jabs about the daily forecast and offer friendly remarks: Still waiting for that drizzle to show up! Or: All this dust—if I'd known, I wouldn't have washed my car yesterday. If she wasn't on their team, they'd best weaken her. They'd loosen the earth under her feet, just in case, so it would be easy to pull out if needed.

Her strained foot muscles signaled to her that she had inadvertently sped up her pace. Dogs barked boldly in the distance. It wasn't fair: the mistakes they found in her forecast weren't mistakes. She'd clearly written "chance of drizzle," and they'd read, "drizzle"; "possible haziness," and they'd focused on "possible." People hear what they want to hear. She was precise. And she hadn't pronounced an opinion on the pipeline until she'd thoroughly studied the issue, as was her nature. She read academic articles and watched a few publicity and nature films aimed at the general public. She was especially taken by an image of massive walruses whose marine ice was melting, as they searched for a place to rest and had no choice but to crowd onto a steep, rocky island. They managed to climb up onto the island, using their tusks as stakes and dragging their bodies up. But when they tried to get back into the water they tumbled down, heavy bags rolling uncontrollably downhill until they shattered on the craggy rocks.

The pipeline might be enough, she finally said with some hesitation. For a while. For the time being. But her words had no effect: they'd already made up their minds.

When the late-spring floods arrived, the water ran through the pipeline, briefly visible, frothing as it came down from the mountains and disappeared into the pipe's mouth and onward, under the town, like a diffident butler serving a dish and quickly retreating to the servants' quarters, knowing his place. They could watch it fearlessly, enjoying the spectacle of natural forces without concern for the damages they might inflict.

The road stretched out beneath her feet, desolate.

Far on the other side of the planet, hurricanes formed and meteorologists tracked them and gave them human names.

Very nearby, in the scrubland, environmental activists counted and recounted the gazelles. Deep below it all, tectonic plates kept up their perpetual motion, which had begun before it all and would continue long after, a motion imperceptible yet quantifiable.

The woman walking on the main street kept close to the shadows cast by the houses, trying not to gauge the touch of the air on her skin at around twenty-three degrees. Just walk and walk, all the way to the end of the street.

She had an old habit, and so when her eyes independently noticed that she was getting close to a suitable stone, she glanced around to make sure no one could see, and without breaking her stride she leaned over for a second, picked up the stone, and put it in her mouth. She could guess a stone's flavor and texture based on its appearance. This one was gray and full of tiny pores, the kind one should move around one's mouth for a long time, from side to side, to feel the effervescence, and at just the right moment crack it and allow its taste to fill one's mouth.

As a toddler she'd often gnawed on stones and plaster. The habit came and went, especially tempting after the rain, when the smell of the earth seduced her to savor and swallow everything. She stopped when she grew up, but had recently been drawn to it again. Once, twice, just to explore what it was. And again for the third and fourth times. The flavor of the smell. The aroma of earth and water and air together.

When she was a child, she thought she loved these forces of nature, that she and they were on the same side, supporting each other. She assumed they were her home, in this town and its untamed surroundings. She knew them, and they her. When she went to college to study earth sciences, she still thought in terms of comprehension and adaptation, harmony between man and nature. But recently she'd begun to wonder if a weather forecaster who loved rain wasn't a little bit like a fisherman who loved fish. Whose side was she on? And they, so colossal, so indifferent—did they even have a side?

She peeked at her watch. One fifty. In ten minutes, weather balloons would be released at the same time in eight hundred places around the world, as they were every day. Humidity, pressure, and temperature would be measured in the sky, the atmosphere would be profiled, air currents and cloud movements would be determined. Everything needed to prophesy the next day.

One fifty was undoubtedly afternoon. They must be down in the canyon by now, at the lower opening of the duct. Taking care of the problem.

On dry summer days the local kids were drawn to the pipeline. It started east of town, before the mountains. They liked to sit next to the opening, which was covered with a metal grate, and yell into it to hear their voices echo back. They leaned on the concrete walls meant to block the flow into town and divert the water into the pipe. They could hide behind the walls to make out and smoke cigarettes and dream.

When the weather warmed up, they were spellbound by ties of aversion-cum-attraction to the wailing that erupted from the pipe opening. It transpired that when currents of warm air rose up through the pipe, it emitted a doleful, grievous howl. She began to forecast the sound, half-joking half-serious, exploring the chances of anabatic winds and reporting: This evening will be warmer than usual, with prolonged wails of lamentation. Quiet at night.

No one thought it was funny.

Strangely, these forecasts seemed to connect her with the howling, as if she were partially responsible for it. They incriminated her. Ever since the chilling sound of relentless mourning had begun, the looks of pleading or disappointment they gave her had taken on a hint of warning. A veiled threat: You'd better watch out. Write only what we want to hear.

They wished to silence the howls. Her niece had told her about it last night in the kitchen, as she packed crackers and a bottle of water in her backpack. "We'll go past it on our hike tomorrow. We'll start at the mountains and at midday we'll go down into the canyon. He's going to bring a simple cover, and we'll install it on the pipeline's outlet." She spoke casually. Her eyes were evasive as she dug through her bag. "It's a kind of lid with a one-way opening. If floodwater comes down it will easily push it open and the water will flow, but the wind from below won't be able to get in. You said the air currents from down below are what make the howling sound, right?" She stopped what she was doing and looked straight at her aunt. Her eyes still contained a desire for her blessing. Perhaps she was even hoping she could repair her aunt, enlist her, and everything would be like it used to be. This whole summer had been so different. More complicated, although also more exciting. She was growing up.

"It's a good solution, isn't it?" She tried to make her aunt agree, to make her belong.

219

But her aunt only sat at the table sipping tea. Finally she nodded, but neither of them was sure in response to what.

Green Eyes had already recruited volunteers for this kind of project in the past: they'd spent days building a fence around the gazelles' habitat, to keep the wild dogs out.

The pack of dogs had been spotted more and more frequently. And it seemed to be growing; there was talk of seven or eight individuals, with newly abandoned dogs joining and some born into the pack. They ran around together, found scraps of food, hunted rodents, and recently they'd isolated a gazelle from its herd, surrounded it, and attacked.

Once, from a distance, she thought she'd seen her dog in the pack, the one who'd been swept away in the flood. But that didn't make sense. Could he have survived, a pampered domesticated dog who'd been helpless without her, accustomed to constant care? The dog she saw, who'd stopped walking for a moment, had an unusual black spot on its neck, a shape that resembled an open human hand, just like her own dog had had. But from afar it was hard to tell the marking from dirt. He'd looked at her for an instant and then turned and left.

From a distance now, again, she heard the barking. Even if it was just local pets, she found herself thinking it might be the wild dogs. After they'd been shut out of the gazelles' area, there were increased incidents of them coming into town, and once they were spotted in the vineyards, starved, lurking for a toddler who'd wandered away from his parents.

She listened attentively to the barks. Since seeing the dog with the black marking, she'd sometimes tried to pick out his voice among the din, and to remember how he'd acted. If he'd survived, how had he been integrated into the pack, what was his status? She tried to reconstruct the way he'd been standing relative to the other dogs when she'd seen him, what his body language meant, whether it attested to a position of power, of influence. Or was he just one of the pack, perhaps rejected, marginalized. If it was him at all.

The dogs no longer sounded that far away, all barking together. She picked up her pace. Had they already installed the cover? How long would that take, how would they attach it to the concrete? It was hard to know what they'd decided to do, especially since she'd opted not to interrogate, to be less and less involved, not to make decisions. She'd only heard about them culling the dogs after the fact, too. When she thought she heard gunshots at midday once, she still didn't know. Later that evening she walked around the outskirts of town, in the vineyards near the gazelle fence, looking closely into the dusk. She thought she saw something on the ground, perhaps a carcass, but then a pair of green eyes appeared opposite her. Now you can walk around here freely, he said with a grave nod. We've put that trouble behind us.

She didn't ask, but he explained that they'd left part of the pack unharmed. They'd only curbed it, curtailed its strength. He might have said that they'd hit the leader. It was a humane solution, he noted. What did he mean—that they hadn't killed any dogs but only stunned and relocated a couple? Maybe they'd taken them to be trained and adopted? Had he explained who this leader was? After he left, she realized she hadn't been capable of listening because she'd kept thinking about how even in the dark his eyes were narrowed. Open only halfway, as if he were blinded by the scant light.

She'd gone home that night without seeing what it was out there on the ground, walked through the orchards and then the streets for a long time, the town much larger than it had been in her childhood. Immeasurably larger.

Last week, on the porch, when her niece had asked if it would rain on Saturday, she'd shaken her head no. Her niece wanted to know, for Green Eyes, for everyone, if a flood was going to come down from the mountains, enter the pipeline, and burst into the canyon. She wanted to know if it would be dangerous to finish their hike and shut off the howls.

She had not shaken her head because she knew for certain that it wouldn't rain, but because she wanted to say that it was impossible to predict a week out. Except that she'd had a stone in her mouth. They were facing each other on the porch, eating dinner, and at a moment of distraction she'd picked a loose piece off the rock wall behind her and quickly put it in her mouth. Her niece had asked her once, surprised—do you have candy in your mouth? And since then she'd been cautious, but this time she'd forgotten. When her niece looked straight at her and asked if the weather would cooperate, she had no escape and no way to take out the stone, which was larger than she'd expected. "Will there be a flood?" the girl asked again, her face full of expectation. And reverence, still.

So she shook her head—no.

Then she bent over for a moment as if she'd dropped something, spat the stone into her hand, and put it on the wood floor. Just as she straightened up, the howling began and quickly died down. She shivered, but her niece's face lit up: she was excited about the hike, about the positive action, the initiative, the warmth of solidarity. "You should come too," she said. "Why don't you join us? It's for everyone." She waved her arm in invitation, as if asking her to sit around a campfire with them. As if she were still a member of the human race.

The heat beat down on her hat, but she kept marching. There was no longer any shade on the street. In this sunlight it was hard to believe it was raining in the mountains not far away. But in fact, you could easily see the swollen cumulus clouds pouring down on the horizon. The sight surprised her, as if she herself had come to believe her own forecast: bright, even in the mountains, no threat of floods. She sped up, confused and unsure of herself. It was hard to see the floods coming because they advanced silently, and by the time they got loud it was too late. She'd said there would not be a flood, so would there or wouldn't there? The colors of the synoptic map swirled in her mind's eye.

She untied the plaid shirt from her waist and put it on, to protect her arms from sunburn. Fair skin like hers had never been right for this region. In fact, it turned out that her entire body was unsuited to this place, unable to feel it, or to identify the winds, the clouds, the creatures. She'd been deceiving even herself. And if that was the case then perhaps everything was fundamentally untrue. It had never really been her home, her skin belonged to a different climate, her forefathers had invaded this place, it was not her body's natural landscape, nature was trying to tell her, to tell them, crudely: You are all immigrants here. Surrender, acclimate, or go back to where you came from.

But where was that?

She could see the edge of the main street, which ended in

a void at the cliff overlooking the canyon. In fact, she admitted to herself, this was not the first time she'd tailored her forecast to the audience's request. She'd started in the summer, but the deviations were usually minor, insignificant. At least until the fall. She wanted to offer them justice and consolation, because the howling was unjust. They'd tried so hard, built the concrete pipeline, cared for the gazelles, the grapes, the dogs, the children, each other, they'd made an effort, and yet it howled and lamented as if they'd done nothing.

The stone in her mouth was ready now, and she cracked it, primed for the smell, the flavor, earth-water-air. But the stone was tough and the taste that spread through her mouth was one of blood. She felt around for the pain with her finger. A broken tooth. She spat and wiped her bloody finger on her overalls.

The dogs sounded close now. They were barking madly. Where was everyone? Were they all on the hike? Had they all gone down to silence the grief? Then why were the dogs barking—were they going to be shot again? Was someone else?

Her tongue was drawn repeatedly to the fracture in her mouth, scratched by it.

She was very close to the edge now, to the cliff, but she hesitated and stopped. She considered turning back. Why go over there? What would she see that she didn't already know from here?

A shutter was suddenly opened in the house next to her. Was someone watching her, scrutinizing to see which way she'd choose to walk?

Without looking, she started to run.

She soon heard steps chasing her. More and more joined in. And more. Many feet, galloping.

Out of breath, she got to the end of the street, to the precipice. This was where the town turned into nature, melded with it, as they liked to proudly explain. But that was a lie. There was nothing to glorify about this connection between the town and its environment, as if it mattered, as if it existed. As if there were two here: town and nature. As if they were not one. Because after all, this street would collapse into the abyss one day and be reunited with it. The footsteps behind her were extremely close and she turned and found herself face-to-face with the dogs. There were at least ten of them. They circled her. She immediately recognized the one with the black spot.

She held her hand out and he came closer and sniffed her palm. The blood on her pants. He gave her a harsh look. Then, repulsed, he took a step back and rejoined the circle. In his eyes she saw no rebuke. And indeed, how could she be blamed, when even Noah hadn't been able to hold back the flood and save everything? No, her dog was not barking to protest her failure to protect him, her allowing him to be swept up with a pack that gave him a life of freedom, with all the hardships and pleasures it brought. The other dogs' penetrating looks also did not lament their abandonment by human beings. On the contrary: in their eyes she saw only fury and disgust at everything that had come before, at the domestication of them. At the domestication of everything.

Her dog grunted and bared his teeth. He hadn't crossed over to the wild side. There were no sides. When he'd allowed himself to be swept away, he'd simply stopped denying what he was.

The other dogs grunted and bared their teeth too. They walked toward her, narrowing the gap. She took a step back. Behind her, from the deep ravine, there rose a soft rustle that was growing louder, and a marvelous, seductive smell of earth that had been dry for a long time and was now being watered. She took another step back and fell like rain.

# Contributors

**Farkhondeh Aghaei** is one of the leaders of a highly successful wave of women writers in post-revolutionary Iran. She harnesses magical realism to express feminist themes and explore class divides. Following an initial burst of productivity in the 1990s, Aghaei's acclaimed literary career—which treats topics as diverse as the transgender experience and religious persecution—began to face opposition from state censors. Her novel *Zanī bā Zanbīl* (Woman with basket) was finally published in 2015 with significant cuts to the original manuscript after languishing under review for nearly a decade.

**Bakhtiyar Ali** is a prolific Kurdish novelist, essayist, and poet born in the city of Sulaymaniyah in Iraqi Kurdistan in 1960. He began his career as a poet and essayist but later established himself as an influential novelist. He was unable to publish most of his work before 1991 due to the strict censorship under Saddam Hussein. In 2017, he received Germany's prestigious Nelly Sachs Prize, marking the first time the prize was awarded to a writer working in a non-European language. In 2016 his novel *Ghezelnus u baxekani xeyal* was published in English as *I*

*Stared at the Night of the City* in Kareem Abdulrahman's translation. It was the first Kurdish-language novel to be published in English. Since the mid-1990s, Ali has been living in Germany.

**Shirzad Alipour** was born in 1989 in Sardasht, Iran. After graduating with an MA in English literature in 2013, he began teaching English. He is a voracious reader of English literature.

**Brian Bergstrom** is a lecturer in the East Asian Studies Department at McGill University in Montréal. His articles and translations have appeared in publications including *Granta, Aperture, Mechademia, positions: asia critique,* and *Japan Forum.* He is the editor and principal translator of *We, the Children of Cats* by Tomoyuki Hoshino (PM Press), which was longlisted for the 2013 Best Translated Book Award.

**Basir Borhani** was born in 1990 in Oshnaviyeh, Iran. He has an MA in English literature and was assistant editor of fiction/essay in translation for *Hamshahri Dastan* magazine from November 2015 through August 2017. His Farsi and Kurdish translations of short stories, literary essays, and memoirs have been published in various literary magazines in Iran. He currently lives in Iran and works as a freelance translator of English, Kurdish, and Farsi.

**Dorota Brauntsch** studied journalism at the University of Wrocław and the Danish School of Journalism in Aarhus. Her photography and reporting project "Ceglane Domy" ("Brick Houses"), documenting the vanishing traditional brick houses of the Pszczyna region of Silesia, was covered by major Polish news publications including *Polityka* and *Gazeta Wyborcza*. In 2017 she received a fellowship to expand that project into her first book, *Domy bezdomne* (Homeless homes), which was published in 2019.

**Sean Gasper Bye**'s translations from Polish include *The King of Warsaw* by Szczepan Twardoch and *Ellis Island: A People's History* by Małgorzata Szejnert. He studied Polish at the School of Slavonic and East European Studies in London and spent five years as literature and humanities curator at the Polish Cultural Institute New York. He is a winner of the *Asymptote* Close Approximations Prize and a recipient of a National Endowment for the Arts translation fellowship.

**Allison M. Charette** translates literature from French into English. Her most recent translation, *Return to the Enchanted Island* by Johary Ravaloson, published in 2019 by AmazonCrossing, is only the second novel to be translated into English from Madagascar. Allison received an NEA Literature Translation

Fellowship in 2018 for her work on Michèle Rakotoson's novel *Lalana* (The road). She also founded the Emerging Literary Translators' Network in America (ELTNA.org), a networking and support group for early-career translators.

**Jessica Cohen** was born in England, raised in Israel, and lives in Denver. She translates contemporary Israeli prose, poetry, and other creative work. She shared the 2017 Man Booker International Prize with David Grossman, for her translation of *A Horse Walks into a Bar*, and has translated major Israeli writers including Amos Oz, Etgar Keret, Ronit Matalon, and Nir Baram.

**Deborah Dawkin** trained as an actress and worked in theater for ten years. She has written creatively and dramatized works. Her translation of Hanne Ørstavik's *The Blue Room* was published by Peirene Press in 2014 as part of the Coming of Age series. Other translations include *To Music* by Ketil Bjørnstad, co-translated with Erik Skuggevik, nominated for the Independent Foreign Fiction Prize in 2010, and more recently, *Story of a Marriage* by Geir Gulliksen and *The Bell in the Lake* by Lars Mytting. She and Erik Skuggevik have also co-translated eight plays by Henrik Ibsen for Penguin Classics.

**Rachel Farmer** is a translator, interpreter, editor, book reviewer, and voracious reader of anything and everything. She translates from French and German into English. In 2020, her work was longlisted for the John Dryden Translation Competition. She lives in Bristol with her partner and far too many books.

**Gøhril Gabrielsen** was born in 1961, grew up in Finnmark, the northernmost county in Norway, and currently lives in Oslo. Her debut novel, *Unevnelige hendelser* (Unspeakable events), won the Aschehoug First Book Award in 2006. Her second, *Svimlende muligheter, ingen frykt*, was published by Peirene Press in 2015 as *The Looking-Glass Sisters*. *Ankomst*, her latest novel and the winner of the 2017 Havmann Prize for the best book from the north of Norway, was also published in English by Peirene Press, winning a PEN Translates Prize in 2020.

**Erika Kobayashi** is a novelist and visual artist based in Tokyo. History, memory, and radiation play an important role in her work. In her novels, Kobayashi traces the history of radiation via the lives of ordinary people over generations—particularly generations of women: mothers and daughters, grandmothers and granddaughters. Through her writing she wants to make the invisible visible, the unseen seen. Her novel *Madame Curie to chōshoku o* (Breakfast with Madame Curie), published in 2014 by Shueisha, was shortlisted for both the Mishima and the Akutagawa Prize. Her latest novel, the literary thriller *Trinity, Trinity, Trinity* (2019), is about a terrorist attack on the 2020 Tokyo Olympics and examines the intertwined histories of the Olympics, fascism, and nuclear technologies. "Precious Stones" was included in the collection *Kanojo wa kagami no naka o nozokikomu* (She looks into the mirror), published by Shueshia in 2017.

**Andreas Moster** is an author and translator living in Hamburg. His first novel, *Wir leben hier, seit wir geboren sind*, explores the oppression and claustrophobia of an isolated village, as well as the violence bubbling beneath the surface of society.

**Michelle Quay** is a scholar, translator, and research fellow at the University of Birmingham where she works with the GlobalLIT project on Persian literary theory. She has taught Persian at Columbia University, University of Cambridge, and UCLA. A Gates Cambridge alumna, she holds her doctorate in Persian literature from Pembroke College, University of Cambridge. Her literary translations have appeared in *Asymptote Journal*, *World Literature Today*, and *Exchanges*, among others.

**Michèle Rakotoson** is one of the most critically acclaimed authors in Madagascar. She is a master storyteller, one who can just as easily dress herself in the garb of a French writer as a Malagasy one. In addition to her writing, she focuses most of her time on championing the next generation of Malagasy writers, by organizing readings, salons, and conferences in Madagascar. In 2012, the Académie française awarded her its Grande médaille de la Francophonie.

**Tamar Weiss-Gabbay** is an Israeli author. She has published five books in Hebrew, both for adults and children, and has earned rave reviews. Her recent children's book was chosen to be distributed to preschools throughout Israel. She leads various literary-social projects, including The Israeli Women Writers' Forum, Two: A Bilingual Project for Arabic and Hebrew Contemporary Literature, and the street libraries in Jerusalem.

CALICO

The Calico Series, published biannually by Two Lines Press, captures vanguard works of translated literature in stylish, collectible editions. Each Calico is a vibrant snapshot that explores one aspect of our present moment, offering the voices of previously inaccessible, highly innovative writers from around the world today.